BENNY
AND BABE

EOIN COLFER

miramax books

HYPERION PAPERBACKS FOR CHILDREN
New York

For Noreen and Billy

Text copyright © 1999 by Eoin Colfer

For information address Hyperion Books for Children,
114 Fifth Avenue, New York, New York 10011-5690.

Originally published in Ireland by The O'Brien Press Ltd.
Reprinted by permission.
First Hyperion Paperbacks edition, 2007
1 3 5 7 9 10 8 6 4 2
Printed in the United States of America
Library of Congress Cataloging-in-Data on file.
ISBN-13: 978-1-4231-0284-7
ISBN-10: 1-4231-0284-3

Visit www.hyperionbooksforchildren.com

CONTENTS

PROLOGUE

Whenever Benny Shaw remembered the summer, fear drained the strength from his legs and set his heart bursting against his ribs. The mere sound of scraping metal sent twinges rippling across his knee. *Close one, Benny me boy, close one!*

A lot of things had happened last summer, not all of them bad. There were the baits, the discos, Black Chan, and, of course, Babe. Benny smiled at the thought of her. They still kept in touch. Sort of. A letter once in a while. Maybe an accidental meeting on the main street if she was in town buying jeans, or whatever else you couldn't get in those culchie shops in the back of beyond. Not a whole lot really for two people who were supposed to be partners for life.

One day in August had put an end to all that. Babe got a look at what he was really like and decided she was better off without him. This was pretty deep thinking for a

1

young chap, but Benny had been doing a lot of that since the accident. It wasn't as if he had anything else to do. It wasn't as if he was going hurling or anything. Benny searched his knee with a magnet till it clinked on to the steel pin under the skin. Nope, it wasn't as if he was going hurling.

Actually, hurling was how the whole thing started. A parentally approved occupation. And one he was good at, too. But trouble is like that. It sneaks up on you quietly. One minute you're enjoying an innocent puck about, and the next, half the Irish Sea is flowing down your throat, and there's a one-eyed mongrel dog hanging off you.

It wasn't real hurling anyway. It was culchie hurling. And in culchie hurling, the rules are a bit different.

1

CULCHIE HURLING

Duncade was the best place in the world. A small fishing village nestled in the cliffs of southern Wexford. The cove was dominated by Dugan's Tower, a lighthouse named for the Welsh priest who'd hammered Christianity into the locals. Tourism was not encouraged, and the privileged group of annual visitors was sworn to secrecy. It wasn't everywhere that leaning over a quay wall spitting after the tide was considered an honorable pastime. Nobody wanted to jeopardize that. Benny was one of the lucky few. Because his Granda was the lighthouse keeper, his family was accepted as legitimate guests by the clannish villagers.

The Duncade boys had put together a couple of hurling teams. Not full size or anything, just eight on eight. Or more accurately, eight boys on six boys, a girl, and a dog. They came up to the lighthouse looking for Benny, seeing as he spent every daylight hour bashing a ball against the gable end.

"Okeydokey," said Benny with a big innocent look on

his face. After all, how good could these farmer boyos be? Probably spent most of their time running drills with cows and sheep.

"Don't worry, Ma. I'll go easy on them," he roared up the lighthouse's spiral staircase.

His mother muttered in response, too immersed in the day's artistic endeavor to waste any words on her eldest son. Jessica Shaw was a drama teacher with a real passion for her subject. Her current obsession was poetry. She spent hours in the light room thinking of fancy words for sea and clouds.

I mean, poetry, for God's sake, fumed Benny. Cat, bat, and mat. What was the point of it? If you want to look at the sea, go over to the window and have a look. If you want to describe it, buy a camera. All this sorrowful waves and angry clouds bit was for people who were useless at hurling, and therefore had meaningless lives.

Like, for instance, his little brother George, aka the Crawler. He was his mother's boy all right. Sitting out on the rocks communing with nature. Benny threatened to let his boot commune with Georgie's backside if he had to listen to any more poems. His latest act was poetic sentences. Whatever the little eejit said had to rhyme. And he refused to answer at all until he thought of a good one.

"George! Come in for your tea!"

"I can't wait / for my plate."

"Shuddup with all that poetry stuff, will ye?"

"I must rhyme / all the time."

"I'm warning you. Y'see that fist?"

"If pain I feel / I will squeal."

Enough to drive a person mental. At least you could be certain there'd be no sign of the little pest at a hurling match. Georgie considered sport in general to be the pastime of savages.

"He who hurls / is a churl."

Benny wasn't sure what a churl was, but one day he'd find out and then, Crawler beware!

The Duncaders were sitting on a famine wall, chewing hay and kicking cowpats, among other wooller occupations. Benny flattened his cowlick and ambled over, nonchalantly hopping a sliotar on his hurley.

"How's she cuttin' there, men?" he said, using the vernacular.

"Shaw, boy! That's a nice stick you have there."

"Sure it's a grand bitta wood," said Benny, really laying on the accent.

A big massive barn of a chap stood up. Benny swallowed. He'd thought the fellow was already standing. "Holy God, Paudie, you're after sprouting."

Paudie was only fourteen, a year older than Benny himself, and already the size of a round tower.

"Must be all them bales of hay you're throwing around."

"S'pose."

Paudie hefted a hurley the length of a telephone pole. Jagged nails poked out of the rusty bands at its base. There was a dark stain on it that looked suspiciously like blood.

"I'm on your team, am I?" said Benny.

"S'pose."

Benny swallowed a relieved sigh. "Good stuff. Are we right then or what?"

He climbed over a steel gate. The struts were drooping like an old clothes hanger from the passage of a million others too lazy to open the catch. The surface of the pitch left a lot to be desired. There seemed to be a bit of a fairy fort in the center of the field, and the odd sheep was searching for edibles among the scutch.

"Ah here, Paudie. You can't even see the other goal. Would you boys ever get your act together?"

"A bit tough for ye, is it, townie?"

The voice came from below his sight line. Benny glanced down. What appeared to be a pixie was glaring up at him. The creature spoke again.

"I told ye, lads. No guts."

Benny would have spluttered a denial, if he hadn't been afraid of a fairy curse or something. Then the pixie took off her woolly hat and flicked her hair out of her eyes.

"God!" said Benny.

"What?" said the pixie.

"Ah . . . nothing," muttered Benny. What was he going to say? *I'm sorry, young lady, but I mistook you for a mythological creature?* Benny may not have been Mr. Millennium, but he was no gom.

"Well, let's get the show on the road then," said the pixie, twirling a midget hurley like some kung fu baton.

"Fine by me."

"Sure ye don't want to scamper off home for a helmet and some pads?"

"Keep it up now." Benny just knew his cowlick was standing at attention.

"And what? There's no ref here, boy."

Benny rolled his eyes skyward, demonstrating, he hoped, what an immense feat of patience it took for him to suffer this strange girl's ramblings. "Paudie! Are we playing or what?"

Paudie swiped playfully at a cowpat, sending it sailing over the boundary fence. Benny winced. There were campers in the next field. "S'pose."

The teams shambled into some semblance of a formation. Benny automatically assumed the full-forward position. They'd probably put some big monster of a lad on him, but sure he was used to that from playing the Christian Brothers School back in Wexford. Some of the juveniles on their team were at least twenty-four.

"Who've I got?" he shouted across at Paudie, who was busy nudging a belligerent ram out of the area.

"Me," said a voice.

Benny looked down. It was the pixie.

"You?"

"That a problem for you, townie?"

"No problem at all, wooller. Just don't get yer head in the way of me hurley."

The girl whistled softly. "I wouldn't be making threats. He doesn't like it."

"Who's that? The pixie king?"

"No. Him." She nodded at a cowpat.

Benny followed her gaze. The cowpat was growling at him.

"That's Conger. He hates townies."

The little mongrel was about the size of a saucepan, and seemed to be made of brown electricity.

"And how does the mutt identify townies? By the smell of soap, is it?"

Benny never did know when to keep his trap shut. The dog seemed to sense antagonism because he aimed his snout at Benny, and closed one eye. The other was a milky blue haze with no iris or pupil.

The Duncaders froze.

"The eye!"

"Conger's given the evil eye."

The pixie shook her head and crossed herself.

"Ah here," snorted Benny. "A devil dog. Get a grip, will yez?"

He noticed a space widening around him. No one wanted to be too close when Conger made good on his voodoo promise.

Benny, being Benny, wasn't convinced. "Never mind all this psyching-me-out rubbish. I've played in Croke Park."

Paudie strolled over, mild annoyance wrinkling his generally blissful brow. "Here, Babe. Keep a leash on the mutt until we start the game." Conger didn't bother giving Paudie the evil eye. He wasn't stupid.

Two things struck Benny, and his mouth went into action before his brain had a chance to paste a government warning over it. "Until we start the game? You mean, the dog's playing!"

Paudie shrugged. So what?

"And Babe. What sort of a name is Babe?"

"Better than George and Bernard Shaw," sneered Babe the pixie.

Benny, for the millionth time, silently fumed over his mother's obsession with literature. Imagine being one half of a playwright's name! For years he'd been trying to think of a comeback for that slur, and he still couldn't manage it.

"Yeah, well . . ." he said, trailing off lamely.

Babe rolled her woolly hat back over a shock of curly hair. Victory was hers.

Benny glowered at her. Babe by name, but most certainly not by nature. You win this battle, Obi Wan, but the war is far from over.

The ball went in. Benny, naively assuming they were playing strategy, held his position. The rest of them bulled into the center, diving into a writhing mass of limbs.

Babe was itching to join the fray. She snapped her fingers at Conger.

"Mark the townie, boy," she commanded. "You know what to do." And she was off, disappearing up to her neck in culchie flesh.

Conger gave a little yip, turning his bandy gaze on Benny.

"What happened to your eye, Conger? Hurt yourself drinking out of a toilet, did you?"

Conger tensed, baring nasty little incisors. That look said: keep it up, townie, let's see what that Wexford leg tastes like.

The tangle of bodies on the pitch was like one of those cartoon frays. Benny half expected to see stars and the word POW appear in fluorescent colors above the dust. Incredibly, it was Babe who emerged with the ball. She was flailing all around with her hurley. Paudie fell, smitten under the chin. He had the glazed look of concussion in his eyes. But then, Paudie had that look at the best of times.

Benny narrowed his eyes against the sun. Time for God-given talent to make its mark. He mapped out the move in his head. Nip in, a little illegal trip for that smart aleck Babe girl—nothing painful, just flat-faced humilia-tion—then scoop up the free ball, and fire it in for an easy point. Or goal, depending on how far it went over the pile of jumpers that were the makeshift goalposts. Simple for a young man of his ability.

Stage one went according to plan. Benny bent low and nipped in toward the culchie stew. Babe tumbled out of the scrimmage just as he got there. Their eyes met. Or rather his eyes met her curly fringe. Benny gave his best vulpine snarl. And the girl made her move.

Perfect. So predictable.

Benny stuck out his foot for the trip. Except there was no girl, just a little lump of dog, chewing on the toe of his runner. Babe had dummied him and was halfway to the other end of the field. Benny didn't know which offended him more: being suckered by a girl, or catching rabies from her mongrel. Squealing like a teething baby, he tried to slap the dog off with his hurley, but only succeeded in bashing himself on the shins. Babe, meanwhile, had tapped the sliotar into an open goal.

Benny soon copped on to the trick of dealing with

Conger—the minuscule dog applied pressure only if you moved. He was forced to stand stock-still on one foot until Babe made her way back from the goal. By this time a whole tribe of culchies was gathered around snickering.

"Laugh it up, farmer boys," said Benny in a friendly tone, in case the dog was sensitive to that sort of thing. "Soon as I get muttley here off me foot, you better watch that goal."

"Problems, townie?" All you could see of Babe's head was hair and a grin.

"Me? No. Everything's fine, thanks very much, except for I'm about to kill this stupid dog if you don't get him off me foot!"

"Be careful there, Shaw. He can smell fear, you know."

"Fear!" Benny squeaked. "Who's afraid?"

He felt a needlelike tooth jittering on his big toe, and willed his pulse to slow down.

Babe sighed. "I suppose I might as well save poor townie from the big bad doggie."

She snapped her fingers again. "Conger! Throw him back."

Conger spat out Benny's foot as though it smelt worse than a barrel of old fish, which in fairness . . .

Benny wiggled his toes experimentally. Everything flexed normally. "Lucky for that dog you did that. I was about to—"

Conger growled. Benny shut up.

By this time Paudie had hauled himself out of the muck.

"One—nil. That was your fault, Benny. Babe is your man. Right, face up for the puck-out."

It was no good. Benny's nerve was gone. It was bad enough being uncertain about whether to flatten a girl or not, but on top of that there was the dog growling every time the sliotar came anywhere near them. He barely won a ball. It was embarrassing. Humiliating. If he'd been a racehorse, they'd have put him out of his misery.

Full time. Six-goal advantage for the opposing culchies. Benny felt like jumping off the end of the quay. Knowing his luck, the tide would be out. He tried to slink off home unnoticed, but Babe was having none of that.

"Hey, townie, going home for a sob, are ye?"

Benny smiled widely to demonstrate just how un-upset he was.

The Duncade girl laughed. "Don't worry, townie. You can play with the juniors next week."

Of course, all the other culchies thought this was hilarious. Who cared which team you were on as long as the townie got slagged.

"Yeah, yeah, yeah," said Benny, painfully aware that this was a pitiful excuse for a smart comeback. Struggling against an instinct to bolt for the lighthouse, Benny casually vaulted the gate and strolled up the sea road.

Usually Benny Shaw considered himself a bit of a wit. Not in a Shakespeare-play fashion, but in a one-of-the-lads-trading-insults kind of a way, but this wall of chuckling farmers totally unnerved him. He needed professional help to deal with these people. Time to talk to Granda.

Paddy Shaw was one of your original mariners. The kind who didn't need instruments to tell them which way was north. In a nautical career that spanned over half a century, Benny's Granda had sailed around the world, captained a deep sea trawler, and indulged in several quasi-legal ventures that some cynical types might refer to as smuggling. He was living out his retirement as keeper of Dugan's Rock lighthouse.

Benny trudged up the spiral staircase and stepped out onto the cast-iron platform. As usual, the view robbed the words from his mouth. Dugan's peninsula stretched northwest to the lights of Wexford and south to Rosslare. Every five seconds the massive light swung around and painted the night white.

The Captain was rolling a pencil-thin cigarette from a pouch of pungent tobacco. The pouch, Granda claimed, was made from the scalp of an Australian who'd tried to mug him in Borneo. It was very unwise to mess with Paddy Shaw. Local legend had it that he had once keelhauled a pot poacher. Granted it had been under a dinghy, but that was only because Granda had been in a dinghy at the time.

"Howye, Granda."

"'lo, boy." Granda struck a match, making a lantern around it with his folded hands.

"How's the tower, Captain?"

Paddy Shaw grunted. "Sure, I don't know. You better ask the computer. All I do is check all the little lights are green."

"Granda?"

"Hmm?"

"Granda, I had a bit of a game today."

"Is that right?"

"Yeah. With the cul . . . with the locals."

Granda chuckled, a phlegmy rumble, full of fags and whiskey. "I see. Got an education, did ye?"

Benny wiggled his toe inside the trainer. "Yep."

"I'm sure it's not the first time ye've had the stuffing pucked outta you. Do you no harm to lose a bit of that cockiness."

Benny nodded patiently, fully aware that adults felt obliged to give a bit of a lecture before actually helping with anything. "There was a girl, Granda."

"Oh, now we're getting to it. Woman trouble, is it? I remember one time in Madagascar, I spied this dusky beauty washing clothes in the river. The problem was that the tribal elders wouldn't—"

"It's nothing like that, Granda. It's just she kept beating me in tackles. Her and her stupid dog."

Granda guffawed. "You've met Babe and Conger?"

Benny nodded ruefully.

"Babe Meara. An Amazon like her mother. Moved down here from Hook Head last winter. Don't get on the wrong side of the Mearas, Benny."

"Too late."

Granda shrugged. "Ye'r living on borrowed time so. Them Mearas are like the Sicilians. Never forget anything."

"What're you supposed to do, though, when a girl is tackling you? I can't just be hopping off her like I would a lad."

Granda turned suddenly serious. "You want to get Babe Meara?"

Benny nodded.

"You really want to get her?"

Benny kept right on nodding.

"Then you've got to play the game her way. No prisoners. She sends one of your team to the hospital, you send one of hers to the morgue. That's the Duncade way, and that's how to get Babe Meara."

Benny frowned. "Granda?"

"Yes, boy."

"You robbed that outta that film *The Untouchables*,

didn't you? Sean Connery said that to Kevin Costner."

Granda was unrepentant. "Robbed it? Sure it was me that used that line in the first place. Them Hollywood fellows must've robbed it from me." Granda said all this with a very straight face, so Benny decided to believe it.

"Right, so. No prisoners."

"That's it, boy. Unless, of course, there's something else going on here besides hurling."

Benny licked a palm and flattened the salt-stiffened ancestral cowlick. "What is it about women, Granda? Why are they so different? Take Ma, for instance."

"A wonderful woman, your mother."

Benny found himself agreeing. "I suppose. But all this drama stuff . . ."

Paddy Shaw lowered himself onto a fish-box seat. He slapped the plastic beside him. Benny sat. Granda pulled off his denim hat, his own gray cowlick sticking up like a vertical pig's tail.

"You're a good man with a hurley, Benny. But you know nothing about women. Your mother is a beautiful, intelligent, spirited lady who won't be led around by any eejit son of mine."

"Granda!"

"Ah, now . . . it's grand for me to call your Da an eejit. Just like it's grand for him to call you one."

"Fair enough. But the poetry, that's not normal."

"You have to understand, Benny. Your mother is from Wicklow—Greystones to be precise."

"So?"

"Greystones is very close to Dublin. Do I have to spell it out for you?"

Benny shook his head. The peculiarities of Dubliners were well documented.

"It's a them-and-us thing," continued Granda. "We can't understand what your Ma brings to the family, we can just be grateful to have it."

Benny looked doubtful.

"I suppose you'd be happier to have a mother ironing your shorts, slapping up your dinners, and having no life of her own?"

To his surprise, Benny realized that he wouldn't.

"Don't try to understand city dwellers, son, but do try to avoid taking a check from one if at all possible."

"Thanks. 'Night, Captain."

Paddy Shaw ruffled his grandson's hair. "'Night, Bosun."

Benny stepped in out of the night, climbing down the spiral staircase to his room. Take no prisoners. He didn't know if he could flatten a girl. Then he remembered Babe Meara's snide chuckle, and he thought that maybe he'd find the resolve somewhere. And if that little dog bothered him again, he'd be sailing over the hedge like one of Paudie's airborne cowpats.

2
CHILDISH THINGS

Benny was basically a loner. It wasn't that he preferred it that way. He just seemed to have a knack of alienating people before they got to know the sensitive person under the smart aleck. Way, way under.

And though Benny made no effort whatsoever to actually make friends, it didn't stop him feeling sorry for himself because he had none. A large part of his day was spent silently berating the people responsible for his problems. There was Da for packing them all off to Duncade while he got to stay in Wexford. Then there was Georgie for not conforming to Benny's idea of a little brother, which was more or less a ball boy. Ma was in the bad books for writing poetry with Georgie and ignoring Benny. And finally he was moody with the people of Duncade in general, for being a shower of farmers who didn't appreciate him for the hurling prodigy that he was.

Every morning he would fume away for a good ten

minutes before loping downstairs to sulk at the breakfast table. The morning after the hurling disaster he was particularly touchy.

"Not fair."

Jessica Shaw held back the urge to tip the jug of milk over her eldest's head. She would, as her own mother had always advised, offer it up.

"What's not fair, honey?"

"Nothing."

"Good. Eat your breakfast."

Benny was tempted just to stop whining and enjoy the fry-up. You didn't get one of those every morning, and the rashers were perfect. Crisp enough to break. But he just couldn't resist the opportunity to voice his sorrows.

"There's nothing to do here, Ma."

Jessica Shaw's eyebrow arched. "Ma, Bernard? Don't use that low-down—"

"Sorry—Mam. I'm bored."

"Bored?"

"Yes. Bored stiff."

"Because, if you're really bored—"

"I am. Stiff as a . . . really stiff." Not being a literary buff, Benny never could finish a simile.

"As it happens, I'm planning a reading of some of my latest poems this morning. Collectively entitled 'Nature the Leveller'."

Benny paled. "Ah . . . I dunno, Ma—sorry, Mam. But I have to go and . . . I'd love to and all, but there's this yoke. So maybe later, okay?"

Jessica smiled. The best way to make Bernard forget one problem was to give him another. She watched bemusedly as her eldest son crammed a hearty fry down his gullet, terrified he'd be asked to clarify his flimsy excuse. Not that there actually was a poetry reading. Still, there could be if Bernard didn't make himself scarce after breakfast.

Benny was still chewing going out the door. The depression of loneliness was nothing compared to the brain-stewing boredom of sitting through a poetry reading. He would go down to the dock and indulge in his shameful secret pastime.

Benny Shaw had turned thirteen two weeks previously. He was a young adult destined for the CBS Secondary in just under two months. And Benny Shaw had a dark secret. Deep in the pocket of his threadbare combat trousers was . . . a Special Forces Action Figure. Should this fact ever be discovered by a living soul, the mortification would probably be fatal. Action figures were for age four to ten. Anyone over that age caught in possession of such a figure would be deemed a big girly sissy who played with dolls. Not a nice epitaph to have carved on your tombstone. *Here lies Bernard Shaw, who is chiefly remembered for disgracing all males by playing with action figures at the age of thirteen. He was also a hurling all-star, but that is rendered null and void by the doll-playing episode.*

Benny knew it was wrong. He knew he'd have to emigrate back to Tunisia if anyone found out. But he couldn't help it. Major Action listened to him. He nodded his little head sympathetically, and swiveled his beady eyes in an understanding manner. Also, you could burst Major Action off any conceivable surface and he wouldn't break. He hadn't so far, anyway. But today was the big test. If the Major came through this one, he could get a promotion.

Benny scratched the doll's tennis-ball hair. "Take it easy in there, big fella."

Another curious thing was Benny's adoption of a passable American accent whenever he spoke to Major Action. His mother would have been thrilled at the dramatic tendencies.

Benny passed the old timers spitting streamers of tobacco over the quay wall. Granda was wedged in the middle of them, his huge hands held high and wide. Looked like he was telling about finding the Holy Grail again.

George was down on the slip, marshaling a group of urchins into a line. Benny paused for a moment to check a theory.

"One, two, three," said Georgie. "Now, all bow together."

Benny snorted. Yep, everything his brother did annoyed him.

He strolled up the avenue to the old manor house, into what was left of the Duncade Castle courtyard. Most of the stone had been cannibalized by locals over the centuries, until only the main tower itself remained. Scheduled for restoration, it had been closed to the public for years. Only a ground-floor room, used by fishermen to store lobster pots, remained open.

Benny climbed the outside steps and hauled a manky fish box away from a chimney flue. He held his breath and ducked inside. The chimney was wide enough for a person to climb up to the second floor, if you didn't mind the dark or the possibility of laying your hands on some fresh cat droppings. The children of Duncade had been using this secret entrance for years. They were far too resourceful to allow a padlock and a few bars to keep them out of an actual Norman tower.

Of course you were in deadly danger every second you spent in Duncade Castle. The mud floor covered a multitude of sinkholes that could drop you fifty feet in a minute. The battlements were liable to collapse on your head at any moment, and the arched windows were just wide enough for a sarcastic little teenager to fall through. Local legend had it that Granda's buddy, old Jerry Bent, had plunged from the tower on his eighteenth birthday.

From that day to this, all Jerry could utter was the word "butterflies."

Confident he was now alone, Benny pulled the doll out of his pocket.

"Time to see what you're made of, Major."

The Major didn't answer because he was terrified. (Being a doll might also have had something to do with it.)

A spiral staircase led to the tower roof. Several steps were missing, and it was a favorite pastime of the older boys to spit down on whatever poor unfortunate was making the climb behind them. Benny hopped over the gaps, imagining what it must have been like for the Celts trying to overrun a tower like this. Cramped, weighed down with weapons, not able to see more than three feet in front of you, and expecting an armored knight to split you with a mace at any moment.

Benny followed the shaft of light ahead until he emerged on the roof. You had to stay on the battlements here because the floor was sunken and crumbling from the center outward. Every year there was less holding this story up. Granda predicted that the whole thing would collapse within the decade.

Benny peeked out between the crenellations. It was pretty high. Jerry Bent was lucky he could even say "butterflies." There was a spectacular view, but Benny didn't waste a moment appreciating it. For him there was only one view, and that was from the top of the lighthouse.

"Right, Major. Zero hour."

Benny attached the parachute to Major Action's gripping hands. It was a homemade sort of a parachute. An old dishcloth and some worn laces. But Benny had seen a program about skydiving once, and he was confident he'd absorbed enough information to overcome the effects of g-force. How hard could it be?

If Major Action could have spoken, he would have screamed for mercy. *Oh for the love of God, please don't hurl me from this altitude, you demented Irish devil.* Unfortunately, he was as mute as Benny at volunteer time in speech and drama class.

"Any last words? No? Good. Fly, Major Action. Our hopes and dreams fly with you."

And over the side went poor Major Action. Benny stuck his head out between the limestone blocks to follow the doll's trajectory. The parachute was not performing as expected. In fact, it seemed to have wrapped itself around the Major's plastic frame and decreased his wind resistance.

"Hmm," said Benny, scratching his chin in scientific contemplation.

Benny's role playing stopped abruptly when he noticed two figures climbing the tower's outside steps.

"No!" he gasped.

Fate couldn't be that cruel. It was that odious girl Babe and her mongrel. They were standing directly under the reluctant paratrooper's estimated point of impact.

"No," he moaned. "No, no, please no."

Benny would have added a few Hail Marys to his plea, but there was no time. The humanoid missile struck. Benny had read once that a penny dropped from the Eiffel Tower would impact with the destructive power of a bullet. He wondered what an action figure would do.

The doll clattered Conger on the side of the head. Spooked and dazed, the mongrel stepped sideways. Unfortunately, that brought him into midair, as they were halfway up the steps at the time. His fall was broken by the rancid contents of a bait barrel, full to the brim with salted guts and fish heads. Conger went right through the wooden lid, and up to his neck in fish bits.

"Oh no!" Benny breathed, a manic giggle threatening to erupt from his throat. It was funny, really, when you thought about it. It'd be a lot funnier if the girl had gone down. Now, there was something he'd pay real money to see.

Babe jumped off the steps and hauled Conger out by the collar. The dog began to lick himself clean, then stopped as the brine bit into his tongue. His injured howl split the peaceful Duncade air, and the unfortunate animal set off like a bullet, in search of fresh water.

Babe started to follow him, but paused. She bent to

pick up the doll, casting an accusing eye skyward.

Benny whipped back his head, wishing his heart wouldn't beat so loudly. You never know what sort of powers these culchie pixies might have. When he finally allowed himself to sneak a peek, the girl was nowhere to be seen. Doubtless off to find her distressed pet.

Benny grinned. There's no revenge like anonymous revenge. It was well worth an old bit of plastic to see that mutt getting a slime bath. Poor old Major Action. Lost in the line of duty.

He trotted over to the rooftop doorway. Babe Meara would be investigating the scene of the crime as soon as Conger managed to scrape his tongue on some rock. He had no intention of being here when she returned to transform the culprit into a toad. Whistling merrily, Benny danced down the spiral staircase. He was getting too old to be playing with dolls anyway.

Another favorite pastime in Duncade was fishing for crawlies. These were the pygmy versions of the cruel clawed crabs that scurried along the seabed in deep water. Traditionally, crawlie fishing was the jurisdiction of the under tens, but once again, in his loneliness, Benny was regressing to the activities of summers gone by.

First you chipped a barnacle off the rocks with your knife. Then you prized the unfortunate crustacean out of his house, pale flesh contracting between your fingers. Benny used to have nightmares about the ritual, imagining high-pitched screams of anguish emitting from the shellfish. But after the violence of playing against Enniscorthy CBS, this was small potatoes.

You skewered the barnacle with a threepenny barbed hook, and lowered him, still squirming, into the water. Charming. Benny had used the same line since Granda had given it to him nearly a decade ago. Ten-pound-strain catgut, with a streaky marble weight. Benny was convinced it was the stone that brought him luck. An almost perfect sphere with a hole clean through the center. Very rare. Granda said he'd got it out of the belly of a tiger shark in the South China Sea. He explained how the stomach acid had burned away the soft rock. It was a deadly story, so Benny decided to believe it.

Of course, being a teenager, Benny couldn't just stroll on to the slipway and lower his line in broad daylight. Certainly not. He might as well suck a pacifier and wear a bib. No. Much like the action figure experiments, this had to be a covert operation.

Late that evening, under cover of darkness, Benny loaded up with tackle and headed over to the inside dock. The slip was deserted, all rugrats long since consigned to their little beds. The tide was about half in, still well below the slime line.

Benny sat on the edge of the long ramp, feet dangling above the water. Time to sacrifice a shellfish. He slid a barnacle along the side of his live bait bucket. The poor little chap was sucking desperately but couldn't get a grip on the plastic. Working his penknife blade down, Benny popped him out of his shell, like jelly out of a mold.

Benny lay on his stomach and hung his torch from a rusty nail on the side of the slip wall. A circle of light pierced the surface of the water and meandered wavily to the bottom. Benny uncoiled his line into that circle.

The theory behind catching crawlies is that they have more brawn than sense. Once they clamp their claws on to a tasty morsel they will not relinquish it, even when being hauled out of their environment by a being two hundred times their size. It's not the hook that gets them, it's their own stubbornness.

Benny jiggled the bait around in the pool of light. He imagined the crabs tuning in to the barnacle's dying spasms. Any second now, they would come scurrying out of the weeds into the sandy patch.

A claw poked out from behind the husk of a dead spider crab. It snipped at the light suspiciously. Benny gave the bait a little tug, sending fleshy microbes scurrying through the water. The claw stiffened. Message received. The crawlie revealed itself. A big sucker, about the size of a baby's hand. The shell was dark, almost black, with orange dots sprayed across it. Nasty little fellows. They'd have your finger off given a chance.

The miniature crab's eyestalks zoomed in on the fish sacrifice. Benny could almost see them widening at the thought of an unexpected feast. It scurried sideways from the marine undergrowth, nearly overturning itself in its haste to claim the meat.

Benny tugged the bait out of reach purely to annoy the shellfish. Outraged, the crab scythed the water, snipping floaty tendrils of pale meat. Benny wondered if this was like the *X Files* for fish, with him being the alien. Maybe that's what all aliens were. Big lads with torches. While Benny was off in philosophy land, the crawlie made a moonwalk-type jump through the glowing water. In slow motion he arced upwards and latched triumphantly on to his prize.

The catgut strained against the creases in Benny's fingers. These little fellows were stronger than they looked. He reeled in the line slowly, winding it around a yellowed finger bone. Granda swore that a Japanese man had presented him with this bone as atonement for siphoning petrol from his outboard.

The crawlie fought all the way up, yanking grimly on the recently deceased barnacle. The meat would not be dislodged, pinioned in place by the reverse barb on the hook. Still, the crawlie persevered, scattering the torchlight with its thrashings. Gently, Benny swung his catch out of the water and on to the slick stones of the slipway.

The diminutive crab noticed something was amiss. It spun around in a tight circle, periscope eyes searching for a possible threat. They landed on the two-hundred-claw-high land mammal.

"That's right, crusty," said Benny. "You're on my turf now."

But it was all talk. Benny wouldn't even pick up the little crab, never mind harm it. He'd just chase it around the slip for a while, then herd it back into the water. It could grow old and terrify its crawlie grandchildren with tales of the great two-legged giant.

They circled each other like David and Goliath. The crawlie lifted its pincers high, snapping furiously. Ah, thought Benny, a ninja. This chap wasn't one bit afraid. Probably a psycho-bully crab. The other crabs were more than likely hoping that Benny would do them all a favor and squash this chap with a giant foot. Sorry, boys, this one gets thrown back.

But it didn't get thrown back, because a crazed, one-eyed mutt pounced on its back, cracking it like an eggshell.

"God almighty!" yelped Benny, tumbling back onto his behind. But the shocks weren't over yet. Before his brain had recovered from the trauma of crab guts and gnashing teeth, his eyes sent another horrific image to be dealt with.

It was Major Action! But the swine had tortured him. His spiky hair had been singed off, and he was missing an arm.

"Major!" squeaked Benny.

Babe Meara stepped into his field of vision. "So, you know the doll's name, townie."

Benny considered it. Screaming the doll's name out loud would certainly point to him owning it. "Eh . . . no. I was just saying . . . major, as in 'major bummer.' It's a town phrase. You woollers probably wouldn't have heard it."

"Go on, ye big liar. Major bummer, get out of it."

Benny was quite chuffed at being called big. "How do you know it's mine? Some pixie telepathy, is it?"

Babe sneered. "No, Shaw. Smell."

Benny shook his head in mock disgust. "That soap giving me away again, is it?"

"No, gom!" shouted the Duncade girl, taking a swipe at him with the remains of Major Action. "Conger tracked you from the scent."

Benny guffawed. "Conger! That mongrel. He couldn't track a cow in a barn."

Benny was going to add a few more items that Conger couldn't track, but he sensed a blue eye being focused in his direction.

"So, it's not your little girly doll?"

"Absolutely not," lied Benny. "On my honor as a Cub

Scout." He made a vague gesture that he hoped approximated a scout salute.

"Sure?" asked Babe sweetly.

"Certain," he replied, an uneasy feeling churning his stomach.

"Okay, then." Babe clicked her tongue, and dropped Major Action on the slip. Conger released the mangled crab and pounced on the unfortunate doll. For several minutes Benny had to sit and nonchalantly watch his childhood friend being mutilated by the frantic canine. It was tough, but the alternative was his own flesh in those jaws, and that would be a whole lot tougher. When the durable plastic had been thoroughly cracked and pulverized, Babe clicked her tongue again.

"Conger," she commanded. "Throw it back."

The dog dropped Major Action like a burning coal. Babe picked up the doll's remains. "You're certain this isn't yours?"

Benny swallowed. "Certain."

Babe pulled her arm back. "Then you won't mind when I do this!"

The Duncade girl lofted Major into the middle of the slip. Water flowed through his dozen new perforations, and he sank like an anchor.

Benny watched the impact circles spread across the harbor, lapping against the trawler hulls. What could he do? If Babe had been a boy they could have had a fight or something. Even if she were a proper girl, he could have insulted her dress. But she was this weird tomboy creature, even scruffier than your average single farmer.

What had Granda said? Take no prisoners. Make a stand or be harassed forever. It was bad enough being bullied, but bullied by a midget! So Benny decided to take a stand, but as usual his methods were a bit extreme.

"Aww! Is the little townie feeling—" began Babe.

That was as far as she got because Benny had grabbed her bobbly hat and fired it into the water. "Now!" he gloated. "Can yer farmer hat swim? It would appear not."

Babe was speechless. She rubbed the top of her head as though the hat would reappear. "I . . . you . . . that was my . . ."

"Sorry. I don't speak wooler. Only English." The final insult.

Babe's little face twisted in anger. "Conger! Kill!"

Oops. The dog's eyes widened with glee. His paws clicked on the flat stone, accelerating across the slipway. Benny crouched low, determined not to be out-maneuvered by the mutt again. Conger leaped. Benny twisted sideways. The mongrel flew past, teeth chomping the air where his enemy used to be. Benny gave him a boot in the hind quarters for good measure. The unfortunate dog spun tail over ears into the water, landing with a splash that would certainly have earned him a 9.5 in competition.

Babe blindsided Benny, grappling him below the knees in a flying tackle. Benny had had worse. He'd had fellows land on him so hard he'd made a face cast in the mud. This wasn't so bad. He was about to chortle derisively when his feet went out from under him. They had strayed below the tide line, and the rock slime was as slippy as wet soap. They went down in a tussle, rolling over and over till their feet were flailing in the dark waters.

"Okay," panted Benny. "Okay now, Meara. Take it easy. One false move and we're both in the quay."

"I do know that, Shaw," retorted Babe. "I'm the one that lives here."

They grasped each other's shoulders, inching onto their knees.

"What's your problem, Babe? You've been harassing me since you first laid eyes on me."

Babe glared into his face. "My problem? You're the one with the problem. Swanning in here with your 'culchie' this and your 'farmer' that. Asking for trouble."

"Sure, you are culchies. I'm a townie. So what?"

"You assaulted my dog!"

"He fouled me in the match!"

"He's a dog! He doesn't know the rules!"

"Shouldn't be playing then!"

They stood on shaky legs, still hanging on to each

other's sleeves. It was almost like two friends on new skates.

Babe sighed. "Listen. Conger, you know, he can get a bit excited."

"You're telling me!"

"I'm trying to be nice here!"

"Okay."

"So?"

"So what?"

Babe scowled. "So, have you anything nice to say?"

"Em . . . Well, I'm sure whoever dropped that doll on Conger was only playing around and didn't know you were there at all."

Babe smiled. Benny realized the castle incident had never been mentioned. He'd confessed.

"Fair enough. Apology accepted."

"Good. Now, can we get out of here?"

Conger scrabbled on to the slip. He was annoyed. You could see it in his eye. Babe watched him nervously.

"Conger, sit!"

Conger did not sit. He shook himself vigorously, spraying a sheet of water over the humans.

"Oooh. That's freezing!"

"Conger, sit! I'm warning you!"

The dog was gone beyond warning. He was on a mission of revenge. The master-pet relationship was on hold.

"Conger! There's a good boy."

Conger did not look like a good boy, not the way he was baring his fangs at Benny.

"No, boy! No!"

The dog tucked his head down and charged. Babe and Benny stood powerless to evade the canine aggressor. It is a terrible thing to know your fate and be unable to avoid it. In slow motion, Conger launched himself into the air, blue eye glittering.

Conger crashed into them, a missile of bone and teeth. Benny caught Babe's eye. She was laughing. Benny laughed too. Then they were bowled over, and their mouths filled with diesel-impregnated salt water. The two of them stopped laughing immediately.

Benny squelched up the lighthouse drive. Granda was having a late roll-up on the bench.

"'Night, Bosun."

"'Night, Captain."

He eyed Benny's clothing. "Babe?"

Benny nodded ruefully. "Yep."

Granda chuckled and spat. "I knew a woman once in Brindisi, when I was spying during the war. Italians are very fiery, y'know. Temperamental. Her brothers tied me up, tortured me about the Allied invasion date. "Do you expect me to talk?" I said. "No, Mr. Shaw," they replied. "We expect you to die.""

Benny did the math. Granda must've been the only spy in nappies. Plus, he was pretty sure that torture bit was out of a Bond movie. But there was no point interrupting. Benny was stuck there, shivering, until this story was over.

"So this Italian lady, Maria. Whenever she saw me, she'd go out of her way to humiliate me by any means possible." He looked Benny in the eye. "Turns out that was her way of looking for attention. Being vindictive was supposed to make me start looking in a direction me eyes wouldn't usually bother with. Do you get me?"

Benny nodded politely, ducking inside the lighthouse. What sort of a story was that? No ending or anything. You wouldn't even call it a story. Just a couple of sentences. Granda was slipping.

Benny was halfway up the stairs when the point of Granda's tale hit him. Looking for attention? No. It couldn't be. Babe Meara? She hated him. Hated his guts. And he hated her too. Her and her dopey dog . . . Except for that one second just before they fell into the water, when she smiled. Benny was shocked to find himself grinning. Wise up, boy! That wasn't even a real smile. It was hysteria. Babe Meara hated anyone who came from anywhere there were more people than animals. And he should stop mooning around on staircases thinking about her. The only thing that could come out of that was pneumonia.

3

PAX

Benny made a solemn vow to himself. That was it with the baby stuff. No more dolls or crawlie fishing. He was only asking for trouble. From now on it was hard teenager-type activities. Time to grow up.

Benny sought out the Captain after breakfast on Sunday morning. He was down at the quay wall spitting after the tide—a time-honored pastime among Duncaders. It was also considered the civic duty of all mature mariners to loiter on the dockside deriding every craft tied up at the harbor wall. This was not, they would argue, gossiping, as their observations could possibly save lives one day.

Benny sidled into a space between Granda and Jerry Bent. The pair of them were singularly unimpressed by a fiberglass pleasure boat from Dublin.

"I mean, look at it, will ye?" said Granda, spitting in the boat's general direction. "Force five—no, force four and it's gone."

Jerry nodded sagely. "Butterflies," he replied.

"I mean to say, there's no ballast, and that pump hole's the size of a pin."

"Butterflies."

"You'd be better off trying to bail out the QE2 with a Tayto bag." Granda took boats personally. A nonfunctional craft in his harbor was seen as an insult to all sailors. "Dubliners, I suppose."

Jerry rolled his eyes. "Butterflies," he said with a distinct Dublin lilt.

"Sure, them fellas wouldn't know a boat from a septic tank. All they can tell you about is golf—every one of them's a great golfer. But what're they doing here, I ask you? Are there any golf clubs around here, Mister? I'll give them golf clubs."

Benny nodded sympathetically. "Golf clubs." He chanced a spit at the offending craft, but only succeeded in dribbling down the front of his sweatshirt.

"Don't be embarrassing me, boy. Watch."

Granda rolled a big spitball around the back of his throat, then launched it in a smooth arc over the wall. It was classic comet formation. A globule of main body, complemented by an aerodynamic tail. You had to be impressed by that.

"Now you, Bosun."

Benny psyched himself up. The pressure was on. He

coughed up a big wad of liquid from the back of his throat, and closed his lips tightly over it.

"Good boy. But remember, volume isn't everything. You need projection. Compressed air is the trick."

Benny nodded, building up the pressure in his mouth. His cheeks ballooned and he let fly, sticking out his chin for good measure.

"Not bad," admitted Granda, following the spit's progress into the shallows. "You have to work on your distance. That and nonchalance."

Jerry cleared his throat.

Granda rubbed his hands. "Oh, now ye'r in for a treat. The master is giving an impromptu performance."

Jerry tested the air with a finger and pursed his lips.

"Usually Jerry doesn't spit in public outside competition," whispered Paddy Shaw.

There was a soft putt, and a bulletlike mass sped from between Jerry's lips. It moved too fast for human eyes to follow, but a nearby seagull squawked and fell off its fish box perch.

Jerry winked proudly. "Butterflies."

Granda punched him fondly on the shoulder. "Shut up, you, and stop your bragging."

This is more like it, thought Benny. Man stuff.

Most young lads have a place where they go and goof off

for hours on end. Benny, naturally, had to have the most cleverly constructed hideaway in the province. Several years ago he'd battered out a hideout in one of the densest patches of ditch in Duncade, extending it annually until the entire bush structure was little more than a shell.

Benny would not allow himself to go there now. Forts were consigned to the mental heap marked "kids' stuff." No more would he crawl on his belly through a tunnel hacked in a ditch. No more would he sit in his hemispherical hideaway, slapping insects off any exposed patch of skin, and definitely no more would he suck splinters out of his knees after a hard day's bush battering. Those days were over. He was a man now.

Instead, he scaled the walls of the salthouse and settled in for a bout of self pity. There was a time when this roof would be lined with young lads, drinking Fanta or throwing Tayto bags full of water at passersby. There was only Benny these days, though. The rest of them were pressed into service for the summer. Paudie was picking spuds on his uncle's farm. Seanie and Sean Ahern were on the trawler, and Furty Howlin was still in reform school. Deserters, the lot of them.

The salthouse was a long, one-story building, where salt had been extracted from seawater by peasants some time in the colonial past. Generations of Duncaders had used its overgrown roof as a natural gathering place.

South facing, angled and padded by moss, it was the perfect vantage point for summer lounging. The steep climb gave it the added attraction of inaccessibility to adults and little kids. There was an unspoken rule: no one went on the salthouse until they were at least twelve, or until they could beat up someone who was at least twelve.

Benny was trapped in limbo. In between generations. Next year a new shower of youngsters would claim the salthouse, but for now it was only the young fella whose Da didn't have him working for the summer.

Benny pulled a telescope out of its holster on his belt and pointed it out to sea, hoping to spot a few boats. The trick to operating this instrument was slow sweeps. Anything faster than five degrees a second would result in blurring. His gaze landed on the Ahern craft—a manky rust bucket that had never been painted as far as Benny could remember. A crust of scales and guts covered ninety percent of the hull. When the Aherns were tied up, you didn't have to see their boat, you could smell it.

Seanie and Sean were hauling a train of lobster pots. Their Da, Big Jim Ahern, was on the gaff. It was backbreaking work. Big Jim would snag a buoy with the hooked gaff, then the two lads pulled up twenty fathoms of drenched rope until a weighted pot appeared on the gunwales. More often than not a worthless spider crab would have poached the bait, and be sitting there with a big guilty head on him. After some mighty cursing, the Aherns would tie in some salted bait, smash the spider crab against the hull, and fire the pot back into the depths.

They'd taken Benny on the pots once. In spite of all their derogative townie comments, he'd managed to snare a buoy on the first pass. He was just giving the Aherns a cocky wink when the slack gave out on the pot line and wrenched the gaff out of his grasp. The heavy steel cap sent it spiraling into the depths. Naturally, the gaff was a family heirloom. Handed down through generations of Aherns. Originally used by Smugglin' Jack Ahern to drag caskets out of the surf. Big Jim had to go drinking for a week after the loss of it. Benny was not taken on the pots again.

Something was skittering along the rocks by the Babby's Pool. Benny swung his lens back to the movement. It was Conger, the little chap going ballistic. Where was the midget pixie? Benny scanned the outcrop, but there was no sign of her. Then his stomach gave a hump-backed-bridge lurch. Two boots were sticking up out of the weed.

Benny took the scope away, checking what he'd seen with eyes only. They were still there. Two brown boots protruding vertically from a clump of brown seaweed.

"Oh no!" said Benny.

What was that eejit doing to herself? He slid down the

salthouse roof on his behind, launching himself into the field below. He landed running, automatically slipping into a distance rhythm. His heart was bursting against his ribcage with barely suppressed panic. A ridiculous thought popped into his head. He was responsible because he had wished it on her. Not specifically wished, like *I hope Babe Meara drowns in the Babby's Pool.* Just bad things in general.

Benny crested the meadow bordering the rocks. The boots were still there, wiggling slightly. She was still alive! Thank God! He skipped down over the limestone, avoiding anything dark or green. Last thing he needed now was to fracture his own skull in a rescue attempt. Imagine the ribbing he'd get in heaven over that.

Conger heard him coming. He twirled like a canine ballerina, pointing a wet snout at the approaching townie. Benny ignored him, throwing himself across the last few yards of flat rock. Conger sat back on his haunches, miffed at being overlooked. Probably need hours of doggy therapy to regain his self-esteem.

Benny grabbed the boots.

"Hold on, there!" he yelled manfully. "I've got you!"

This statement was accurate only if he was talking specifically to the boots, because they came off in his hands. Those and one Boyzone sock. Two wiggling feet were left sticking out of the weeds. The feet looked annoyed.

Benny sat back, staring at the boots as if a person would grow out of them. He was getting that old familiar I've-just-made-a-huge-blunder sensation. Babe Meara was hauling herself out of a crevice in the rocks. Large strands of seaweed were entangled in her replacement woolly cap, and Benny could've sworn he saw a shrimp in there.

"What do you think you're playing at, Shaw?"

Benny smiled weakly. "Eh . . . I really admire Boyzone for the positive image they present of Ireland."

Babe's face was morphing through various shades of red. "What? Are you simple or something? Is that it? What are you going on about? Boyzone?"

"Your ah . . ." Benny waved Ronan Keating's woolly visage at her.

Babe grabbed the proffered sock. She pogoed around, pulling it back on her foot. "They were a present."

"Oh."

"Anyway, don't be changing the subject, townie! What're you doin' tryin' to murder me?"

Attack, Benny's coach, Father Barty Finn, had always advised, is the best form of crippling the other fellow.

"What am I doing? You were the one with her head stuck down a hole! I thought you were drowning or something."

For a phantom moment Babe's face softened. "You were trying to save me?"

Benny's lip hung down to his chin. "For all the thanks I get."

"Soft eejit," swore Babe, obviously over her tender phase. "You're a Jonah. That's what it is. A walking disaster zone. You want thanks, do you? Well, thanks. Thanks a million. But the next time you see me in mortal danger, just walk the other way. Okay?"

"Count on it."

Benny knew he should storm off in a huff. It would have been the grown-up thing to do. They obviously hated each other, so what was he hanging around for?

"So what were you at, anyway? If you weren't trying to commit suicide."

"None of your business."

"Some big culchie secret, is it? Cloning sheep or something?"

Babe glared at him. "You're a real charmer, aren't you? Probably why you have so many friends."

That was a mean one. Benny decided to pretend he was offended. "That's not very . . ." he began, then hid his face in his hands, overcome.

Babe, being human underneath it all, immediately regretted the remark. "Well, I didn't mean . . . it's just you . . ." The girl scowled, infuriated. She wasn't ready to apologize just yet, but felt she owed Benny something. "You want to know what I was doing?"

"Yes, please," said Benny meekly.

"Well, c'mere, then, and give me a hand."

Immediately mollified, Benny trotted across the flat rock, throwing Conger a nasty look on the way past. A huge wedge of weed was hanging down into the Babby's Pool, so named because legend had it that weak infants were bathed in its sulphurous waters to toughen them up. Babe stretched an arm under the weed, and with a grunt, flipped it back like a duvet.

"There," she said.

Benny peered into the little crevice beneath. Slick sea anemones retracted from the sunlight and a crawlie scuttled for cover. "So?"

Babe sighed. "So, it's a bait trap. A natural lure trap."

Benny's gaze remained infuriatingly blank.

Babe spoke slowly, as one would to a child or simpleton townie. "A trap."

"Yeah."

"For lures."

Benny blinked. "Oh! The lures get trapped in the weeds and rock!"

"Exactly."

"So?"

Babe glared at Benny. "Are you trying to be funny?"

"I don't have to try." One of Benny's standard answers.

"Look, I get the lure bit and all, but the head down in the water bit still escapes me."

Babe rubbed her eyes as though they pained her. "All right, Benny, let's take it from the beginning, will we? Ye thick townie eejit."

Benny nodded. She'd called him by his first name!

"Y'see, every night during the summer, moron townies like yerself come down to the village hoping to catch a few mackerel or pollack for dinner."

"Got it so far."

"Right. So on the way, they stop in the tackle shop and spend two-fifty on a shiny new German lure."

Benny whistled. "Two-fifty. That much?"

"Upon attaching the lure to their line, they fire it out willy-nilly into the high tide until they foul it in the weeds or on the rocks."

"I know. You'd want to hear the cursing out of them."

"So, the new lure is lost, and yer man ends up buying fish off one of the boys on the dock just so's he won't go home empty-handed."

"Your point being?"

"My point obviously being that I find lures at low tide, and sell them back to the boys that lost them for half the price."

Benny chewed his lip. "Isn't that illegal?"

"Nope. Valid salvage. Law of the sea."

Benny nodded. Granda invoked the salvage law for anything left unattended for more than ten minutes. Benny had put a bottle of Cidona in a rock pool once to cool it down and had returned to find the Captain tipping the last drops down his gullet. An expensive lesson.

"I never saw you selling anything."

Babe pulled a leather pouch from her belt. "I don't have enough yet. Here, look."

She unrolled the pouch. Inside, hooked on a hundred tiny loops, was a fortune in salvaged lures. Slim Germans, dull homemade leads, scaled spooners, and rubber eels.

"Not enough?"

"You need a good selection. The customer wants choice. In the Hook, I used to make up to twenty pounds a night. One August bank holiday weekend I pulled in a hundred and twenty-six pounds."

Benny started paying attention. "God almighty!"

Babe knotted the pouch. "You ever tell anybody about these baits and . . ."

"And what?"

The diminutive girl took a complicated-looking knife from her pocket and flicked open the blade. "Guess."

Benny remembered Granda's advice. No prisoners. "Oh, the fear. I'll take that knife off you, and I'll gut you with it. Then I'll gut your dog."

Babe grinned. "I look forward to it, Benny."

Obligatory threats out of the way, normal conversation could be resumed.

"So, pixie. You find anything down the hole?"

"Yes, townie. As a matter of fact I did. Lovely spooner. Can't reach it though."

Benny lay on the rocks, craning his head into the crevice. "Where?"

"There."

He squinted into the forest of weed and water. Dulse and kelp lagged the rock, throwing back a million sun sparkles.

"Where what? I can't see anything."

Babe elbowed him out of the way. "There. Look, you blind gom. By the water-line."

Suddenly Benny did see. Just one more sparkle in the pool. But this one had a red eye. He reached down, scrabbling blindly for the metal.

"Watch out for the—"

"Ow!"

"—hook," completed Babe, trying to swallow a smirk.

"Oh, har de har har, pixie."

Benny's fingers closed around the bait, wrenching it vengefully from the crevice.

"Got it!" he breathed triumphantly.

"That's one pound seventy-five right there in your paw."

"Go on," marveled Benny. "Just like that."

"Yep. Those red-eyes are the top of the range. Only your caster gold will bring in a better price than a red-eye."

Benny shoved a lacerated finger into the side of his gob. "All this money just lying around."

"It's not just lying around. You have to know where to look. As if you would have found anything by yourself with your big townie head on you."

Benny bristled. "I found old red-eye here, didn't I?"

"You did in your dreams! You just picked it up. Hand it over."

"I dunno now. Law of the sea and all that."

"Shaw!"

Benny twirled the lure in his fingers. "You never would have got it without me."

Babe Meara clicked her fingers at Conger. "Red alert, boy."

The little dog crouched like a runner on the blocks, sloppy strings of drool pooling around his paws.

Benny was unimpressed. He was pretty certain he could take the dog. "Now, that is disgusting. Did you teach him that?"

Benny was working himself up to a good old row. One with loads of family insults. But Babe played her trump card. A tiny tear grew at the corner of her eye.

"Ah here," said Benny, disgusted. "Take it if you're going to start whining."

Babe sniffed, hiding behind her hands.

"Go on. I don't want the stupid lure, anyway."

Reaching out a shaky hand, the supposedly distraught girl snatched the red-eye.

"Sucker," she gloated.

Benny glowered. Was this girl ever going to stop dummying him?

That was it. The logical end of their encounter. Seeing as they detested each other, what could there possibly be left to talk about? For some mysterious reason, neither teenager moved from the flat rocks.

"Well?" said Benny.

"Well?"

"I suppose you'll be off up the coast, then. Looking for more buried treasure?"

Babe closed one eye. "Aye, Cap'n."

Benny laughed and was immediately raging with himself. Rule one of the face-off situation: never respond to humor. Women didn't respect that in a man, and it makes you look girly.

"Would you like to tag along?"

Internally, Benny scoffed. Tag along? Not only would he not like to tag along, he didn't even like the phrase "tag along." Sounded like something to do with shopping. You and your psycho dog better go and check into a maximum security insane asylum if you think

I'm tagging along anywhere with the likes of you, Benny thought.

Aloud he said, "That'd be good." And though he'd probably die before admitting it, that was what the human under the smart aleck wanted to say all along.

Babe slumped, the tension seeping out of her. For a second Benny caught a flash of hazel eyes. Then she adjusted her bobbly hat, and was herself again. "Just don't be ruining ecosystems with your big clodhopping feet."

"Me? You're the one with the farmer boots!"

"These happen to be Timberlands. The best rock shoe available."

Benny studied the soles. He was a firm believer in the right equipment. Suddenly his runners seemed awfully flimsy.

"Timberlands?"

"Yep. These lads have pulled me out of a few holes, I'm telling you."

"Hmm," muttered Benny, as if he had any clue about the subject. "Nice grips."

"Good ankle support too."

"How much?"

"Eighty quid."

"Go on!"

"I'm telling you. One week's lure money last summer. Worth every penny."

Benny whistled. If he'd had any doubt about the boots' quality, it disappeared when he heard the price. Anything that expensive must be good.

"One week's money?"

"Yep."

Benny could feel his interest growing. Whatever about principles, he was a sucker for material wealth. The idea of actually being able to buy something worth eighty pounds was a very sweet one indeed.

"So if I was to, like, tag along . . ."

Babe chewed her bottom lip. "Here's the deal. I could do with a partner—four eyes are better than two. That should be obvious even to a . . . even to you. But there's no point taking on a stumbling eejit who couldn't find a lure in a fish's gob. Not saying you are a stumbling eejit, you understand, but there's definite potential there."

Benny squinted. "Was that an insult?"

"So," continued Babe, ignoring the question, "I generally find about a dozen saleable lures a day. If you can come up with, say, six, on your own, then we're partners. If not, it's back to dolls and crawlies for you, townie."

Benny mulled it over. Townie jibes aside, it seemed a decent enough proposition. Surely he could find six lures along the whole fishing coast. I mean, if she could do it, how hard could it be?

"Righto, young one, you're on."

"Good stuff." Babe spat on her palm and held it out. "Shake."

Benny felt his lip rippling. Surely all this hand-spitting stuff went out with the pirates. Still, this girl was wooller through and through. He was probably lucky she didn't want to do a blood-partners ritual.

So he shook, grimacing as the liquid squirted between his fingers. Conger trotted over and sealed the handshake with a slobbery lick.

"And remember this, Benny Shaw," intoned Babe. "Everything I show you from here on is classified information. Tell anybody and . . ."

"I know, I know," sighed Benny, wiping his hand on the rocks. "You'll slit my throat with your knife. How much was that, by the way?"

Every rock had a name, and you could never truly claim to belong in a seaside village until you knew every one of them. Of course it was possible to navigate using the numbers painted on the coastline by the tourist board. But no true fisherman would ever stoop to using those guidelines. Sure, what sort of history could there be in a heap of spray-painted numbers?

So every rock had a name, and every name had a story. When you asked your Granda the name of a particular outcrop, you had to be prepared to listen to the saga that went with it. There was the aforementioned Babby's Pool, with the whole infant-scrubbing thing. And Horatio's Bridge, the natural overpass, where Father Horatio Mac Manus tried to kill himself when caught discussing confessions; one of his parishioners dived into the stormy seas to give him a good hammering before he drowned. Jutting out toward the lightship was Frenchy's Peak. Local legend had it that one of the French fleet landed a few crates of rifles here on its way to Bantry Bay in 1798.

Benny reckoned that seeing as he'd been forced to suffer these stories, it was his duty as an annoying know-all to inflict them on Babe Meara. He could see her mood disimproving with every yarn, and it cheered him up to no end. The great thing about boring people to death is that they believe your intentions are noble.

They climbed down a steep cliff on to a plateau known as Katie's Ribbon.

"Wait till I tell you this one," said Benny, with a big enthusiastic face on him. "Here's where two best friends dueled it out over the affections of a local wench."

Babe groaned. "I don't like that word."

"What? Local? I was just trying to avoid saying culchie."

"Not local! Wench."

"Wench? You don't like wench? Why wouldn't you like wench?"

Conger growled. So did Babe. "Just shut up with the history lesson, would you? I'm trying to concentrate."

Benny was wounded. "But these stories tell us a lot about the area."

Babe lay on the rocks and dipped her fingers under the waterline. "Do they tell us that there's a small undercut running all along the tideline here? Perfect for catching lures?"

"No," admitted Benny. "They don't tell us that."

He prostrated himself, plunging his hand into the water. "Watch out for the—"

"Ow!"

"—hooks," giggled Babe.

"You're hilarious, you are," moaned Benny, withdrawing his hand. A glittering German hung from his index finger. Babe plucked the barb from his fingertip. He squealed involuntarily.

"Go on, you big baby. Why don't you run home and get yer Ma to kiss it better?"

Benny frowned. "Why don't I drop-kick your runt of a dog into the Atlantic?"

"Because the Atlantic is on the other side of the country."

"I knew that," stammered Benny. "I was going for effect, not accuracy." Internally, he cursed never paying attention in geography. Another joke flat on its face. "So, how much for that one, then?"

Babe scratched at a spot of rust on the edge. "Hmm. Been down there a while. Bit of damage. Say, eighty pence."

"That all?"

"Yep. That's about your average. Right, let's do the rest of this ledge."

Benny nodded, lying back down on the rocks.

"Oh—and, Benny."

"Hmm?"

"Watch out for the hooks."

They scoured the coastline for three hours, scrabbling through every rock pool and crevice. They sifted through weed, slid down inclines, and inched into crannies. Benny was in bits by the time they reached Black Chan.

"Look at me fingers," he moaned. "And me trousers are ruined!"

Babe laughed. "Whatever will you do for that cocktail pah-tay."

"Shut up you, ye farmer."

"Go on, you big girl."

Benny noticed that the sting was going out of their insults. It was safe, familiar ground.

"This is hard work, townie. The hours are bad, too. You have to go out with the low tide every day. Could be anything from four in the morning till ten at night."

"There's a four in the morning, too?" said Benny doubtfully.

Babe tapped one of her boots. "Do you want a pair of these or don't you?"

"Suppose."

It would be an adventure, Benny tried to tell himself. Getting up in the middle of the night would be an adventure.

Black Chan yawned before them, a deep horseshoe chasm with shadowy caves disappearing into the rock face. Gannets and cormorants dived into the waves below with precision accuracy, and white striations laced the rock like petrified lightning.

"El Dorado," breathed Babe.

"Wha'?"

"I'd say there's a gold mine down there."

"Why? No one fishes off here, it's too high."

Babe pointed out to the mouth of the Chan. "Y'see there? The little whirlpools."

Benny shielded his eyes against the sun. "Yep."

"Currents. They drag everything right up to the foot of the cliffs. I'd bet there's stuff all the way from Rosslare to Hook Head in there."

Benny leaned over gingerly, peering down the sheer length of the cliff walls. "We're not going down there, are we?"

"We are in our dreams. Every corpse lost on the southeast coast is hung on the rocks in there. I'm not picking through skeletons for a few moldy old lures."

"You're the boss," said Benny, trying to sound a bit disgusted. In truth he was mightily relieved, as Black Chan was the one place Granda had forbidden him to venture.

"No. This is as far as we go. From the Babby's Pool to Black Chan with the low tide."

"Do you know the story of this place?"

Babe groaned. "Give it a rest, would ye, townie. If I want to be bored stupid, I can read a book or something."

Benny started. That was his philosophy exactly. "No, listen. This is a good one. True, too."

Babe snorted. "I'm sure."

"No, really. My Granda told me. He was there."

Babe plonked herself down on the cliff edge, kicking lumps of clay into the abyss. "Go on, then. Amaze me."

Benny sat beside her. This was unfortunate as Conger was already occupying that space. The dog skittered away, yipping a promise of revenge.

"So anyway," began Benny. "You see that big cave down there?"

Babe's eyes followed Benny's pointing finger. "Yep."

"That was like the party cave, ages ago when me Granda was only a sprog. Whenever some big boat ran aground, all the illegal booze would be brought in there for a big party. There were steps cut out of the rock and everything. So one night most of the village was down there, all drunk as lords. Me Granda says even he was plastered, and he was only eight at the time. Only been smoking a few years then, too."

"Any chance of an intersection with the truth at any stage during this story?"

"Gospel. Honest to God. Anyway, there they were, Irish dancing away. Real Irish dancing too. None of your waving yer arms about or anything. When this black chicken arrives into the cave and starts crowing away."

Babe sucked in her lips in an attempt to stifle a yawn.

"Now, as everybody knows, a black chicken is very bad luck."

"Especially if you eat it. Benny, how long is this—"

"Hold on, now. This is the good bit. Granda's ma, my great grandma, grabbed her family and skedaddled up the steps. She was real superstitious. Had a thing about black chickens. But the rest of them ignored the chicken's warning and broke open another barrel of wine."

Conger tried to butt Benny over the cliff edge.

"Five minutes later, a freak wave swept in and flooded the cave. Twenty-seven people drowned. Whoever escaped the wave was pulled down by the whirlpool."

Babe scratched her chin. "What happened to the chicken?"

"What?"

"You know. The black chicken. I suppose seeing as it

raised the alarm, it was hardly stupid enough to hang around."

"It was a chicken! How clever are chickens?"

"This was obviously a gifted chicken."

"That's not the point of the story," snapped Benny.

"Oh, there's a point?"

"The point is that Black Chan is notorious for freak waves and currents, and we'd be mad to go down there."

"Well, you could've just said that instead of frying my brain with boredom."

"Thanks very much."

"Welcome. Now. Down to business."

Babe spread out the day's haul on the grass beside her. It had been a good day. Two rubber eels, a silver spooner, three Germans, two leads, a red-eye, and four spinners.

"Not bad. About a tenner, I'd say. Now you."

Benny gingerly untangled the hooks and spread his finds on the ground.

Slightly less impressive. Two sets of mangled feathers, a lead, the German, and the long hook of a broken spinner.

"Hmm," said Babe. "That's about two-fifty. I don't even sell feathers. Too much trouble, no markup."

Benny sighed. That was it. She'd never want him for a partner now. He hadn't realized how much he'd wanted in on this business venture until the door was slammed in his face.

"Six we said, wasn't it?"

Benny nodded glumly.

Babe shook her head, like a mechanic studying an engine.

"Well," she said at last. "If I give you credit for the red-eye, that makes six. Sort of."

"Great," squeaked Benny in relieved falsetto. "I mean great," he repeated in a manly bass. "So we're partners then?"

"Partners," said Babe, flicking open her knife. "Now give me your thumb."

So at last Benny had a friend. Or maybe *partner* was a better word. God forbid anyone might utter the words "girl" and "friend" in the same sentence. The mortification would be very damaging to his man-about-village image. Benny had little faith in culchie ideologies, but in matters of fraternization with the opposite sex, he had to admit that their system was infinitely superior to the townie one.

In Wexford, all the lads were beginning to hang around the Presentation Convent School waiting for young ones. Missing training and everything! Where was it all leading? Next thing you knew, they'd be squirting deodorant up their sweaters and heading off to ballet class. Then came the hair gel, then a little stud earring! Then going to the flicks to see films without any killing in them. I mean to say, what was the point of that?

The way Benny saw it, females were only interested in fellows that they could turn into girls. They'd have all males wearing skirts, if that wasn't illegal except in Scotland.

Farmer boys, on the other hand, never even acknowledged females in public. If you went to a culchie dance, it was girls on one side and boys on the other. And the females could count their blessings if the fellow asking them to dance had even bothered taking off his calving gloves, never mind washing himself. In a rural disco, you didn't have to ask what someone did for a living, it was written all over their clothes.

Somewhere along the way you pointed out a good-looking girl to your ma and she rang your one's ma, and a wedding was arranged. Then you went out farming or fishing, she stayed home with the kids. No writing of poetry involved.

It was a good system. Proven effective over the centuries. Just his luck to be the son of the Woman Who Would Change All That. Here lies Benny Shaw, son of Jessica, the female who destroyed civilization. Benny also won three All Ireland hurling medals, of course, but this was rendered null and void by the revolutionary-parent thing.

That's why the partnership with Babe was so perfect. Jessica Shaw would be delighted that her little man was hanging around with a local girl. But he, Benny, would know that Babe wasn't really a girl at all, just a sort of a culchie tomboy. I mean, what sort of a girl went on about climbing boots and penknives? If all girls were like that, Benny reckoned, the battle of the sexes would be sorted in minutes.

Benny was drawn home by pangs of hunger. He tramped into the hallway, sucking his pricked thumb, and depositing daubs of weed on the tiles.

"Mam," he roared plaintively. "What's in it?"

Benny deemed it highly unfair that his mother was not at this moment plying him with sandwiches and fizzy drinks. A definite lapse in duties. Too busy improving herself, no doubt.

"Ma! I'm starving!"

Georgie appeared at the door. "He who shouts / is a lout."

"Shuddup you, ye gom!" scowled Benny. Later he realized that clout rhymed with lout, and if he'd said: *Fancy a clout?* George would've been disgusted. With the *shuddup* response, he was just proving the Crawler's point for him.

"I'm not disposed / to keep my mouth closed."

That was pretty good. Disposed, closed. It was so good

that Benny felt obliged to dole out a few punches. He put his hand in his pocket, drawing out a closed fist. "C'mere, Georgie, look what I've got for you."

Poor innocent George scurried over. "What, oh what / have you got?"

"This!" said Benny, planting his knuckles right in the sore part of his brother's upper arm.

"Aargh!" squealed the poor ten-year-old.

"What?" chuckled Benny nastily. "No rhyme for aargh?"

Jessica Shaw, like all mothers, could pick up a genuine shriek of pain from over five hundred yards, and had learned to filter out fakes through years of false alarms. As if by magic, she appeared at the kitchen table. "What's the problem, boys?"

George rubbed his eyes furiously to redden them. "He gave me a dead-arm / that's grievous bodily harm."

"Bernard?"

"Never touched him."

"Bernard!" There was no playfulness in that tone anymore.

Benny had a flashback to his mother's performance as Lady Macbeth. "Okay, so I gave him a minor dig. It was his own fault. He was . . ."

"He was what, Bernard?"

"Well, he was rhyming . . ."

Benny trailed off. Lame excuse. He couldn't believe he hadn't made up something about George destroying the ozone layer.

Mam's frown deepened. "Rhyming? You hit your brother because he was rhyming?"

Benny kept right on digging that hole. "He was doing it on purpose, Ma."

"Ma, Bernard? Ma?"

"Sorry, Mam."

"So, evil George was rhyming on purpose, was he? Surely he must be executed." Mam frequently ignored the Good Parents' rule about sarcasm, specifically the not-using-it part. Benny was sure that was why he turned out such a smart aleck. "George, you evil demon, using the forces of poetry against Saint Bernard here."

Benny sighed. Time to cut his losses. "Okay. Okay. I'm sorry, all right, Craw . . . George?"

Jessica smiled, a toothy promise of punishment. "Oh no, Bernard, my darling. This tendency toward violence must be curbed."

"Ah, Mam. One punch! I barely grazed him."

"You violated his space."

Benny silently cursed his Ma's hippie women's group.

"I see a long afternoon of jobs ahead."

Benny swallowed. He'd better come up with something quick.

"For a start, the bottom ring of the lighthouse needs painting."

Oh the horror. Not painting.

"And then there's the—"

"I met a girl," blurted Benny.

Jessica froze, her list forgotten. "Pardon, Bernard? I thought you said . . ."

That shook you, thought Benny. "I met a girl, Mam."

Jessica searched his face for a hint of fabrication. "A girl?"

For most parents, this is a sentence weighted with foreboding. They instantly envision months of late nights, temper tantrums, and the inevitable post break-up moodiness. Jessica Shaw, however, had been praying for this day for two years. At last her son was displaying some sign of an interest other than neanderthal ball-bashing. She grabbed Benny's hands and squeezed tightly.

"So? What's her name?"

"Babe," said Benny.

Jessica's eyes speared him. "Babe?" she said, through gritted teeth.

Benny shrugged. He hadn't christened her. "Yeah. Babe."

Jessica's bad mood returned like a flash flood. "Women are not objects, Bernard. We are not put on this earth for the amusement of sexist piglets like yourself, too shallow to appreciate anything beyond your own base interests."

Benny nodded doubtfully. This was taking an unexpected turn. "I see . . ."

Jessica advanced on him. "Do you see, Benny? Do you? Because I don't think you do. I think you're quite happy to take your place in the pantheon of stone age men that pass for cultured here on the tail end of Europe."

Benny backpedaled. This was insane. What in God's name was a pantheon?

"Ma . . ."

Jessica's eyes bugged. "MA?"

"Mam, I meant Mam!"

"This girl is not a babe, Bernard. She has a name."

"I know," interjected Benny desperately. "It's Babe. Her name is Babe."

Jessica paused. Sparks of confusion raced around her head. "Her name is Babe? Her actual name?"

"Don't talk to me," sighed Benny. "And I thought Bern . . . eh . . . other names were bad."

"Babe! What a curious name."

Benny felt the sweat of fear cool on his back. "You don't know the half of it, Mam. If this girl wasn't a girl, she'd be a boy."

"But she is a girl?"

"Yeah, Mam. A girl. Swear to God."

Jessica sighed. "Well, fine then. Bring her around for tea sometime."

"Sure thing, Mam," said Benny aloud, while thinking, to borrow one of Babe's phrases: *I will in me dreams*.

"Okay. Good." Jessica wandered off back to the light room, feeling a sudden urge to lie down.

Benny smirked. Once again his lightning confusion-strike had been effective. Plus, Ma had forgotten all about the work detail. Early parole for unexpected behavior.

Georgie tried to edge toward the door.

"Freeze," said Benny casually. They both knew who would win if it came down to a chase. Georgie duly froze. But if you looked very closely, you'd see that his small frame was shivering slightly. Benny sauntered around the pine table, cruelly flexing his fingers.

"You done wrong, Georgie boy. You turned on yer kin. You gotta take yer lickin'." The hillbilly accent was evidence of just how much Benny was enjoying himself. "Seein' as I'm in a generous mood, I'm a gonna give you the choice. Belly or butt?"

Georgie mulled it over, gamely trying to find a rhyme for butt. Eventually he just pointed.

"So be it," drawled Benny. "Now, remember the rule: If you squeal / more pain you'll feel." He was a great man for the irony, even if he couldn't spell it.

George braced himself against the table in a Captain-Kirk-ready-for-impact stance.

Benny considered it. Toe or flat? The toe concentrated

the pain in one point, whereas the flat of his foot distributed the impact. For the kickee, flat was definitely preferable. What the hell, he was feeling magnanimous.

Benny drew back his runner and gave his brother a token whack in the bum. It was more noise than force. Nevertheless Georgie's features twisted in an effort to swallow imagined pain.

"Eight out of ten," said Benny admiringly. "I'm nearly impressed."

George hobbled off, grasping the source of his agony in both hands. At the door he cast a withering glare at his elder brother. Then his eyes widened and the palms of his hands flattened against an imaginary wall. Benny groaned. Not another mime.

"Can't you just pretend you're normal for ten seconds?"

Georgie's fingers curled around an invisible object. It was long and slender, a rifle or maybe a . . .

"Hurley!" shouted Benny, intrigued in spite of himself. The Crawler was good, you had to give him that; he'd even taken air resistance into account.

George took a few swings, whistling softly for effect.

"Oh the big yawniness of it all," sighed Benny.

Then his brother raised his hands high over his head and dashed the imaginary hurley on to the tiled floor. You could almost hear the wood splinter.

"No!" squeaked Benny. "Nooo!"

It was several seconds before his brain reminded him that nothing had actually happened.

George winked with an evil beyond his years. "I'm going to take your precious hurl and wreck it / Just at the moment when you least expect it."

Benny scoured his brain for an appropriate threat, something so excruciating that it would wipe this hurlacide from Georgie's brain forever. But nothing would come except monosyllabic grunts.

"I . . . ah . . . if . . . God . . ."

George shut the door, leaving a falsetto laugh floating in the air behind him.

Benny berated himself silently. You should've used the toe. There's never any smart comments after a good root with the toe. It was a sad state of affairs when a young chap was threatening property damage against his own big brother. George's sick little rhyme echoed in his ears. When you least expect it. Now, when would he least expect it? He stopped himself. If you figured that one out, then it wouldn't be when you least expected it anymore. He'd just have to be on his guard twenty-four hours a day. If the Crawler wanted an escalation of hostilities, that's exactly what he'd get.

4

ARCHENEMY

Being a townie, Benny had a lot to learn about things rural. Even though his family was only a single generation removed from fishermen, he'd managed to dump centuries of race memory in thirteen short years. Benny did not see fit to reserve space in his brain for anything he considered useless, like grammar, respect for others, or his parents' instructions.

His education began at six o'clock one morning when he was smack in the middle of a lovely dream. Benny, being the little hard man that he was, could allow himself to be sensitive only when he was absolutely positive that no one could see him, including himself. When you're asleep, he rationalized, you've no control over anything, and all those girly emotions, sneaked into your genes by your mother, sneak out to haunt your dreams.

So there he was one morning, chewing on the sleeve of his Rupert Bear pajamas, having a decidedly un-macho dream: there was this little bunny sitting on the grass and he was giving Benny a special eco-medal. "For services to mankind, Bernard," said the rabbit in a cuddly cartoon voice. "Thank you, Happy Bunny," said Benny modestly, bowing his head for the presentation.

"You might as well take this with you, too," growled the rabbit. Growled, thought Benny? Rabbits don't growl. He glanced up to find Bunny's benign head morphing into something far more sinister. Something with teeth!

"Take all of these with you!" roared the now monstrous Happy Bunny, gnashing his molars with a sound like crisps being crushed in a bag. The jagged fangs clamped on to Benny's soft flesh, digging down to the bone! Benny woke up squealing.

"Get off!" he howled. "Get off me, Happy Bunny!"

But Happy Bunny would not relinquish his grip, even on this side of dreamland. In fact, his teeth seemed more material than ever.

Benny opened his eyes. Happy Bunny was, in fact, Conger. Beside him stood Babe, with a grin on her that appeared bigger than her head.

"Happy Bunny?" she inquired innocently. "And who, pray tell, is Happy Bunny?"

Benny scowled. He hated the way people went all educated when they were being sarcastic. He was about to fire back a few retorts when several uncomfortable truths assaulted him at once.

Firstly, there was a girl in his room. On top of that, he was wearing Rupert Bear pajamas. Apparently he'd been ranting on about something called Happy Bunny and . . . there was a girl in his room! That one was of monumental importance and definitely worth repeating. The fact that a mongrel scut of a dog was casually nibbling his leg seemed almost trivial, given the circumstances.

Benny tucked the sheet under his chin, attempting to hide his cartoon-character pajamas.

"What are you doing here?" he spluttered indignantly.

Babe's grin widened, if that was possible. "I got fed up waiting for you and Happy Bunny to show up at the dock. So . . ."

"But this is my . . ."

"Your what?"

Benny reddened. You couldn't be saying words like "bedroom" in front of girls. "My . . . private residence . . . area."

Babe roared laughing. A big throaty guffaw that'd make a pirate proud. "Private residence area? What did you do? Eat one of those word books?"

"Dictionaries?"

"They're the ones."

Benny decided to change tack. "How'd you get in, anyway?"

"Helicopter."

"Helicopter? Where'd you get a helicop—"

"Your Granda let me in, you eejit. God, you're not the brightest in the morning, are you?"

Benny threw the sliotar that he kept under his pillow at Conger, and succeeded in whacking himself on the big toe. The dog stood beside its master, adding his teeth to the grin pool.

"Granda let you in?"

"Yep. Told me to come on up. He apologized for you being such a useless waster, and said he was deeply ashamed that any grandchild of his would miss the tide on his first day."

"What tide?" There were still groups of bunnies bouncing around in Benny's head.

"The low tide, townie. It's ebb today. The furthest down for the whole month. We should be on the rocks already."

"You never said," sulked Benny.

Babe shook her head. "I'm not yer Ma."

"Mam," corrected Benny automatically.

"Ma, Mam, whatever. The times are on the radio every night. You're supposed to be at the archway on the stroke of low tide."

"Right," said Benny, trying to seem suitably contrite. How, he wondered, was he going to get this impossible girl out of his room? "So?"

"So are you coming, or have you unfinished business with Happy Bunny?"

"I'm coming all right. I just have to . . ."

"What?"

"Get dressed! I have to get dressed, okay? So if you don't mind?"

Babe grinned. "Aw, is the poor baby shy? Come on, Conger, we'll let the little townie put on his clothes."

Benny bore the teasing silently, relieved that his Rupies remained hidden.

Babe turned back at the door. "Oh, Benny?"

"What?" snapped the groggy Wexford boy.

"Love the pajamas," she smirked, ushering Conger out the door in front of her.

Benny buried his head in the pillow. Maybe he should try waking up again.

"This is too easy," enthused Babe. "There's just too much ammunition. I don't know what to tease you about first."

Benny shuffled along behind her, kicking sods at Conger's behind. The dog easily avoided the missiles.

"There's the doll thing," continued Babe. "And the crawlie fishing . . ."

"Yeah, yeah, yeah."

"Not to mention Happy Bunny."

"Give it a rest, pixie."

"And let's not forget those Rupert Bear pajamas."

"They were a present, all right?" fumed Benny.

But she had him tied up in knots. Babe Meara knew so many secrets about him now she could write one of those exposés: the secret girlie life of Benny Shaw. There'd be a long queue in the bookshop that day.

The dock was deserted except for a solitary fisherman pouring dollops of cement into the bottom of his lobster pots. They stopped to pass comment, as was the custom. Babe stuck a finger in the cement bucket.

"Bad mix there, Clipper," she observed. "The salt water'll rot that out in a few weeks."

Clipper scooped up a handful of the mix and tasted it. "You know, I think you're right, young one," he said, adding a heaped shovel of powder to the bucket.

"That's not free advice, you know, I'll be expecting a lobster dinner for that one."

Clipper laughed. "Will a shrimp supper do ye?"

"It'll have to, I suppose."

They continued past the salthouse, down to the crumbling arch that separated the Duncade seafront from the coastline. The arch was little more than an elaborate stile, that had once provided access to the estate grazing fields.

"This is our spot," said Babe, patting a cobbled bulwark protruding from the arch's base.

"For selling, is it?" responded Benny eagerly, grateful to be discussing anything besides his private humiliations.

"Yep. It's perfect. We lay out the merchandise here.

Put up a little sign, and count the money rolling in."

Benny nodded. The morning was looking up.

"We should be set by the weekend, providing you can get yourself out of bed in the mornings."

"Worry about yourself, Meara. You won't see me for dust."

"We'll see," said Babe dubiously.

They stepped over the low standing stone and began the routine scouring of the rocks. The sun was penetrating the morning haze now and fried little sheets of steam from the weed. Benny and Babe worked the waterline, bending low to the rocks, often scrabbling blindly in deep crevices. They sifted through ropy weed for the glint of a hook. They squatted beside rock pools and scattered the inhabitants by flipping the stones. There were a million places for lures to hide, and always a price to pay for the careless searcher.

By the time they reached Frenchy's Peak, Benny's fingers were trickling blood from a dozen nicks.

"Keep them in the water," advised Babe. "Kills the germs and toughens your soft little townie fingers."

"Not to mention stings worse than a bagful of nettles."

Babe shook her head. "I don't know if you're able for real work at all, townie. We're not even halfway up, and you're crying already."

"Am not," retorted Benny, trying to keep the hitch out of his voice.

Babe picked her way carefully to the point of the narrow outcrop, her eyes darting across the rock face, devouring it piece by piece. Doubtless, concentration was wrinkling her brow underneath all that curly hair. "Well, would you look at this!"

Benny followed her on to the point. "What?"

Babe pointed down into the shimmering green water. "There, look."

Benny looked, squinting past the glare. Two blue strands were anchored below the waterline, disappearing into the depths.

"What are they?"

Babe rolled up her sleeves. "Ropes," she replied, lying flat on the rocks. Her arm broke the surface, instantly turning a ghostly white, refraction separating it from the rest of her body.

"Come on, then!" she said, nodding at the other rope.

Benny stripped off his sweatshirt and dumped it on the rocks; he might not have done that if he'd known how much Conger liked to play with rags. The water was freezing, with the cold-rain surface not yet tinged by the sun. Benny swallowed a yelp, and grabbed at the blue rope.

It was slick in his fingers, weed and shellfish winding greedily around any bare surface. Benny and Babe hauled, the water buoyancy lessening with every fathom. Eventually they dumped it on to the rocks. A thick net, weighted by four cornerstones. Several lures were fouled in its frayed cords.

"I thought so," said Babe disgustedly.

"What?"

"It's a lures' trap. Someone's put this down deliberately to snag lures."

Benny waved his arm around to get the circulation going. "But you said traps were good."

"Natural traps are fair enough. But this is . . . stealing. Whoever planted this is conning those poor townie eejits out of their money. Anyway, it's illegal."

"What about salvage? The law of the sea and all that?"

Babe straightened her bobble. "Salvage is all right as long as you didn't sink the ship. No, we don't want anything to do with a catch like this."

"Oh."

Babe unfolded the longest blade on her knife. "This coastline is fair game for anyone who wants to search it, not just for some young lad who's too lazy to work."

Quickly sawing through the anchor ropes, Babe consigned the lure trap to the depths. Benny watched the net blend with the blue of the sea, then disappear altogether.

"You sure you should be doing that, pixie? Someone went to a lot of trouble to put that there."

Babe smiled dangerously. "Well, if they don't like it, they can come and talk to me and Conger."

Benny nodded, unconvinced. Suddenly Babe was just a young girl, and Conger just a scrawny mutt. He wouldn't fancy their chances against a steak-fed farmer with a grudge. Benny glanced around nervously, certain that some big wooller was going to come bursting across the meadow brandishing a pitchfork. "Let's get a move on, so. The tide waits for no man, or girl, or dog."

But Babe wasn't in the humor for jokes. Not with a bait pirate on the coast.

Thursday was the big day for bait sellers. With the fish-on-Friday custom still so popular in Catholic Ireland, car-loads of eager townies were dispatched by their wives to bring home the bacon—or not, as it were. They arrived in the hundreds, hunters' bloodlust boiling in their veins, weapons of choice dangling from their fists, or threaded through their hatbands. There were telescopic rods, coun-terweighted reels, hand-painted fiberglass lures and lumi-nous deep-water spinners. Anything to sneak an advantage over the poor fish. They strutted down the seafront in designer fishing gear, trying to ignore the group of sea salts propped against the quay wall splitting their pants laugh-ing. No mariner worth his salt would ever take a rod into his hands. These were amateurs. Out firing lines into any old water, hoping to hook something by blind luck. Many of the fish that came in off the rocks were foul-hooked, a barb through their flank or eye. Literally stunned by a flying missile.

Babe and Benny were all set to make a killing. Benny was excited, this being his first major business venture. He had visions of Timberland boots and Leatherman knives. Benny had even painted a little sign. After much deliberation he'd finally come up with the slogan Lures For Sale, and was quite proud of himself.

The afternoon had been spent on preparation. After an overnight soak in spirits, the Germans and spooners had to be buffed up with a soft cloth. Any rust spots were camouflaged with Airfix silver paint, and the homemade leads were scraped with a dull knife to bring up the shine. All legitimate sales tactics; nothing you wouldn't find in any car dealership.

The Meara-Shaw group displayed their stock on an old cork board, painted black to show up the gleam of the baits. Very professional. Now all they needed were a few customers. Of course, before customers, they got locals checking out the new enterprise.

Jerry Bent and Clipper ambled over, trying to look disinterested.

"Well, God Almighty, what have we got here?" exclaimed Clipper, as if he hadn't been watching them set up for the past half hour.

Babe slapped Jerry's hand away from the board. "Hands off. Customers only."

"Butterflies," mumbled the aggrieved Jerry.

"How do you know we're not customers, anyway?" remarked Clipper.

Babe sniffed. "Because if you two old sea dogs wanted lures you'd be up the rocks on your hands and knees searching for them."

Clipper peered at the merchandise, hands behind his back. "Nice bunch. No feathers?"

"Too much trouble," said Benny. "No markup."

"Good man, townie," Babe grinned. "You're learning."

Jerry pointed at a gold spooner. "Butterflies?" he inquired.

Babe tutted. "I'd say now, about one-fifty."

"One-fifty!" exclaimed Clipper. "God Almighty, it's not a bar of gold ye'r sellin."

"Butterflies," agreed Jerry.

Granda was the next over. "Evenin', Bosun. Evenin', Scut."

"Scut?" blurted Benny.

Babe skewered him with a frosty gaze and drew her knife from its sheath. "If you ever . . ."

There was no need to finish that sentence.

Granda nodded at the sign. "Nice advertising. Good location. Could work. God knows, townies are thick enough to buy their own stuff back."

"Hey," said Benny, injured.

"Not you, Bosun. You're only one generation out of the water. The thickness hasn't completely sunk in yet."

Benny was only slightly mollified by this, especially since everyone else was having a chuckle at his expense.

Paddy Shaw scratched the white stubble on his chin. "I used to be in the bait business meself, you know."

"Did you, Granda?" Benny could sense a story coming on.

"Oh yes. Not this sort of thing now, with bits of metal and rubber. I'm talking live bait for orcas."

"What?"

"Killer whales, boy. Killer whales." Granda pulled a cigarette butt from behind his ear and rested against the arch. "There's nothing a killer whale likes better than a baby shark. Live, though. Has to be alive."

Benny was incredulous. "You went hunting baby sharks?"

Granda nodded. "Yep. Down on the Barrier Reef. The Oceanic Institute were looking for a couple of orcas, so we lured them in with a bag of shark babies and then stunned those suckers with tazers."

Babe shuddered. "You could electrocute yourself doing that!"

Granda considered it. "Not if you're wearing rubber boots."

"Rubber boots, how are ye!" sniggered Clipper.

Even Benny was listening now, even though he knew

there was a ninety-nine percent fairy story probability.

"'Course, that little bag of baby sharks would attract a lot more than killer whales. There'd be hammerheads and great whites and tigers. Cannibalism is no bother to these boys. We'd take them with a rifle, and sell the carcasses to local boys for tourist photos."

Benny swallowed. His little sign was starting to feel a bit boring. Granda rolled up his shirt. A curved scar wound across his hairy belly, punctuated by ragged stitch holes.

"A tiger shark took a nip outta me when I was a bit quick going in for a swim." He nodded meaningfully. "That's when they get you, just when you think it's safe to go back in the water."

Babe frowned. "Didn't Steven Spielberg use that line in *Jaws*?"

Paddy Shaw spat a glob of tobacco juice on the gravel. "What? Another plagiarizin' Yank? One of these days I'm going to sue!" You never knew with Granda. People accused him of being dour, but Benny suspected that a wicked playfulness lurked in the deep wrinkles around his eyes.

An hour later, they got their first customers. Two Dubliners piled out of a four-wheel drive and hauled their gear over to the arch.

"Lookit this, Anto," said one. "Bit of yeehaw capitalism."

Yeehaw was this season's word for country person. Benny giggled. Babe did not.

Anto squinted at the lure board. "See that fella, Frank? I think that fella's mine. I lost him here last week."

"Do you have the serial number?" asked Babe sweetly.

Frank laughed. "Serial number? Serial number, is it? Oh she has you there, Anto. Good on ye, girl."

Benny frowned. "I didn't know there were ser——"

He stopped suddenly when Babe patted the leather sheath where her knife was stored.

Anto shook his head. "I dunno now. I think I have enough lures to be goin' on with."

"Pity," said Babe.

"Wha'?"

"Just with you having that expensive rod and all."

Anto swished the rod like a nautical Zorro. "The Oceanmaster Two Thousand. Graphite stem, alloy rings, molded grip, and retractable to a third of its original size. State of the art, children. Kneel before the king."

"Wow," breathed Babe. "That's why it's a real shame about the lure."

Anto waggled a finger at Babe. "Just stop right there. I'm not falling for any of your yeehaw tricks. Don't try to kid a kidder."

"Fine. See you in a couple of hours so. There'll be fish for sale over by the bollards."

"The bollards?"

"Well, you won't be catching anything with those

feathers. They don't look anything like sprats. Fish aren't stupid, you know."

Benny blinked. Granda was always saying that fish were without doubt the dopiest creatures on the planet, with the possible exception of tourists.

Anto was hooked. "You're saying that fish recognize feathers?"

Babe snorted. "Sure they're staring up at seagulls all day. What do you think they're covered in?"

Frank nodded. "Fair point."

"So what would you recommend then?"

Babe considered it. "Well, with the bend on that graphite, you want something heavy for distance, but I'm sure you already knew that."

"Obviously."

"Or else it's like firing a pea out of a cannon."

Benny agreed sagely. "Pea out of a cannon, boy."

Anto frowned, fully aware he was being had. But what the little elf was saying still made a lot of sense.

"So, the bigger the better, then?"

"Definitely, Sir."

Frank rolled his eyes. "Less of the Sir, young one. We're not Americans."

"Point taken," said Babe.

"I presume the biggest bait is also the most expensive?"

Benny shrugged. "As it happens . . ."

"Go on then, ye chancers," growled Anto. "Give it to me."

Babe plucked the red-eye from the board. "That'll be one pound seventy-five please."

Anto counted out the change. "No chance of a test drive, I suppose?"

"Certainly," said Babe. "There'll just be a one seventy-five insurance premium."

Frank plucked a business card from his wallet. "Give me a call when you're finished school. We could use someone like you."

Babe studied the writing. "Lawyers. Crowd of robbers. At least my customers get something for their money."

"Now, Frank!" guffawed Anto. "That's the first time you've heard the truth to your face."

The exchange took place warily, both parties stretching out their hands cautiously. Eventually goods were traded for cash.

"I'll be back if I don't catch anything with this," warned Anto.

Babe nodded. "If you could leave it till tomorrow, I'll sell you the lure again."

Chuckling, the two men climbed the stile and went on their way, Anto threading the red-eye on to his line.

Benny was genuinely impressed. "I'm genuinely impressed," he said.

Babe dropped the coins into her bum-bag. "You see, townie, it's entertainment as well as commerce. The customer has to feel challenged. That chap'll be trying to catch me out for the rest of the summer."

Benny nodded thoughtfully. An occupation where sarcasm was a plus. He was born for this. "Let me do the next one," he said.

"I don't know," said Babe doubtfully. "I haven't weaned the townie out of you yet."

"Ah, go on. We're always being sarcastic in our family."

"Oh all right, then. But only because you're such a pathetic whiner."

Benny scanned the quay. A little girl was approaching, clutching a pretty pink rod that Barbie might use if she were a real person. He grinned craftily. Like taking candy from a baby. The girl stopped at their stall, chewing the tip of one pigtail. Now, your average person might have had qualms about separating a mere child from her money, but not Bernard Shaw. Benny would pry open the hand of a sleeping nun if it meant making this sale in front of his partner.

He knelt down to her level. "And what's your name, little girl?" he said in a bright singsong voice.

The girl regarded him with the ultra seriousness of the under six. "Victoria," she replied.

Benny clapped his hands in a sickening display of

delight. "Victoria! What a lovely name. Now, Victoria, what can we do for you today?"

"I'd like to buy a plastic fishy."

"And we'd like to sell a plastic fishy," said Benny, the smarm dripping from every word. If anyone nearby had been recovering from the nausea of seasickness, Benny's tones could very well have prompted a relapse.

Victoria studied the board. "Hmm . . ." she said.

"You're probably deciding which lure would be prettiest with your lovely rod."

The girl shook her head, pointing at a pink-and-white spinner. "Mine!" she said.

Benny smiled indulgently. "Oh, you want that one?"

Victoria continued shaking her head, blond pigtails spinning like propeller blades. "No! Mine! My fishy."

Benny felt his cowlick spring to attention on the crown of his head. "No, Vicky."

"Victoria."

"Ah . . . no, Victoria. This isn't your fishy. It just looks like the one you lost. There are millions of fishies like yours, just like there are millions of real fish in the sea."

Benny winked at Babe, delighted with this convincing train of logic. Unfortunately, most children have no truck with logic.

"My fishy!" she repeated, a slight lisp whistling through the gap in her front teeth.

"Do you know the serial number?" inquired Benny, a tad testily.

Victoria didn't answer. Instead she flicked the spinner over on the board. "Look," she said. "Vee Bee. Victoria Byrne. Mine."

Benny looked. The initials VB were indeed stamped into the spinner's paintwork. Pretty convincing argument.

"But you see, Victoria," he wheedled. "You lost it, and we found it down a big black hole with sharks and octopussies, so because we were almost eaten, the spinner is ours now."

"Mine," repeated the girl stubbornly.

"Finders keepers."

"Mine!"

"Law of the sea."

"Mine!"

The word grated against Benny's ears like sandpaper on wood. Time to be firm. If you thought about it, he was actually doing the little girl a favor, teaching her a life lesson.

"I'm sorry, Victoria," he said coldly. "It's fifty pence or no plastic fishy for you."

Victoria hit him with big blue eyes at maximum intensity.

Benny felt his resolve waver, but he would not break. "Fifty pence," he hissed through clenched teeth.

At this point the audience would have been yelling boo, had there been an audience.

Victoria turned on the wobbly lip. "Pweeze, Mister."

Benny blinked a bead of sweat from his eye. "Fifty pence," he stammered.

Then Victoria played her trump card. Opening her mouth beyond the limits of the human jawbone, she filled her lungs for volume, and hollered one word.

"DADDY!"

The word swelled and floated across the stillness of the quay. Benny had visions of some manure-daubed agricultural type pulling his arms from their sockets.

Victoria took another breath.

"Here, here!" said Benny, pressing the spinner into her tiny palm. "Take the stupid thing and go away!"

Victoria smiled angelically. "Thank you, Mister."

"Yeah, yeah, yeah," Benny muttered disgustedly. To round off this bout of humiliation, Victoria decided to give Benny a kiss. Unfortunately she couldn't reach his cheek, so she planted one on his bare elbow.

"Ugh! Get away, you urchin!" yelped the slimed teenager.

Humming happily, Victoria skipped off to share her prize with her father. Benny could feel Babe's glare drilling holes in the back of his head. He turned, whining a flimsy defense. "What choice did I have? You saw the letters."

Wordlessly, Babe flipped the other spinners on the board. The letters VB were stamped into each one.

"They all have those letters," said Benny weakly.

"They're Vee Bees you gom," snapped Babe. "That's the company!"

"I thought . . ."

"Oh we all know what you thought, don't we, Conger?"

Conger scratched his ear disgustedly.

Benny moaned. Even dumb animals were sneering at him.

"It's just that you thought wrong. A typical townie trait!"

"How was I supposed to know? It's not my fault all ye culchie women are devious!"

"We're not devious; we just have brains!"

Benny cradled his head in his hands. At least Granda hadn't witnessed his mortification. Through his fingers, he risked a peek across the quay. There were four people at the fishermen's bench. Granda and Jerry were rubbery with laughter, and Clipper was handing some little girl a nice shiny coin. The little girl was clutching a pink fishing rod.

"This is good," muttered Babe.

Benny was incredulous. "Good?" he spluttered. "Good! Are you from another dimension, pixie!"

"Your Granda is doing us a real favor here, Benny."

Benny couldn't speak. There weren't the words.

"It's a country thing," explained Babe. "You see, technically we're blow-ins. By playing a trick on us like that, they're showing everyone that they don't mind us setting up shop."

Benny was unwilling to give up his sulk. "Couldn't just tell us, I suppose."

Babe punched him on the arm.

"Hey!"

"That's for saying country women are devious. Now, sit down, shut up and behold the master at work."

Benny did as he was told. Words like "behold" always reminded him of his Ma and so inspired automatic obedience.

Babe was indeed a master. She could squeeze blood out of a stone, or cash out of an Enniscorthy man, which was the next best thing. The trick was communication. Sell a laugh and a joke along with the lure. Never be mean or nasty, no need for anyone to feel small. And every time someone claims to have lost one of your lures the previous week, act as though it's the first time you ever heard that one.

By dusk they were out of everything except homemade leads. People, even townies, were reluctant to pay for something you couldn't buy in a shop. And in the poor light, you wouldn't see a lead lure in the bottom of the bath, never mind under ten fathoms of murky salt water. Still, Babe plucked them off the board in turn, smoothing the nicks with some fine emery paper.

"We'll shift them," she muttered confidently. "There's always an eejit just dying to spend his money."

Benny wasn't listening. Firstly, because not listening when someone was talking to him was a bad habit of his. And secondly, because he was watching a shadowy figure strolling down the quay front. He knew that walk, lazy and confident, stopping to kick any pebble, can, or dog that came inside the strike zone. The youth stepped into the buzzing glare of Duncade's one street lamp and nodded thoughtfully at the stall.

"Shaw," he said.

"Furty," answered Benny, stretching his mouth into some semblance of a smile. "I thought you were in . . ."

"Reform school?" Furty leaned on a bollard and began burning ants off the top with his lighter. "No. I did me time and now I'm . . . reformed." He smiled hugely. "Obviously."

"So . . ." said Benny. "How've you been keeping?"

Furty hoisted himself on to the bollard. "Grand, Shaw. Grand. I've been keeping meself busy. Doing a bit of lure hunting actually."

Benny swallowed. Not him. Not Furty Howlin.

"So, up I go the other day to haul in me trap, and there it was—gone."

Benny attempted an innocent shrug. The resulting spasm resembled an electric shock convulsion.

"Now, first of all I blamed me own knots. Maybe I

should have put another hitch on the ropes. But now that I see youse two all cuddled up nicely together, I'm starting to think that ye might have had something to do with it."

Benny bristled. "Who's cuddled?"

Furty smiled coldly. "Don't bother trying to change the subject on me. I know what you did, and I'm not going to forget it."

Now, Benny was quite prepared to lie his way out of this little fix. It was a tried and tested solution which had proved successful for him many times in the past. A little lie hurts no one, he always said, and a big one could actually do some good.

"Hold on there, Furty," he began. "I have absolutely no clue what—"

Benny never got the opportunity to finish his denial, because his belligerent little partner decided to stand up for them.

"Yeah, we cut it, Furty, or whatever your name is. So what?"

Furty blinked, unaccustomed to such blatant defiance, especially from what appeared to be some sort of fairy.

"So what? I'll tell you so what . . ." Furty paused for a moment, uncertain which of his standard threats would be most effective against one of the wee folk. "So now we're enemies, and I'm going to do whatever I can to get my own back."

"Oh, the fear!" scoffed Babe.

Benny groaned. When you came up against a big neanderthal fullback, you went around not through. "Furty. Can we talk about this for a second?"

"No!" shouted Babe.

"No way, boy!" echoed Furty.

"I'm not talking to some jumped-up pirate," stated Babe.

"What?" spluttered Furty.

"You heard me! No real sailor would ever stoop to bait traps."

Furty's eyebrows knitted together in a frown. He was no fool. He knew exactly where he was. Down on the quay with Shaw's old storyteller grandfather staring over at him. No, Furty boy, he told himself. This is not the time. So, instead of launching himself at the two blow-ins, he took a deep shuddering breath and calmed down. If there was one thing he'd learned in Saint Julian's Home for Young Men, it was to bide his time.

"Pirate, is it? That's a good one. I'd say now, that you two are the pirates. Coming in here, stealing what's mine."

"Afraid of a bit of competition, are you?"

Furty snorted. "A townie and a little girlie. I don't call that competition."

Later, Benny couldn't remember what came over him. But he felt this irresistible urge to defend Babe even though Howlin wasn't saying anything he himself hadn't thought a hundred times. He jumped to his feet.

"Babe is not just some little girlie, Howlin."

No more first-name terms now. The lines were drawn.

"Is that a fact?"

"Yes! She's more of a man than you'll ever be." Benny winced. That didn't sound quite as heroic as he would've liked.

Furty laughed. "That makes her three times the man you are."

Babe interrupted their little multiplication argument. "Just shut up, the pair of you," she snapped. "Listen you, there's plenty of coastline and eejit townies to keep us all going. You don't have to start looking on our stretch. And if you do want to start something, then you'll have more than me to deal with. You'll have Conger too."

Conger did his evil-eye routine, tensing every sinew in his tiny frame, and aiming the blue orb in the enemy's direction.

"Him!" chortled Furty. "That little runt. I'll show you what I think of him." He bent down and selected a sharp-edged stone.

Babe glowered at him. "You wouldn't dare!"

"'Course I wouldn't," said Furty, spinning the stone in Conger's direction. It clipped the little dog on the rump, toppling him down the arch steps. The dog scrabbled to his feet and skittered off over the stile. Babe nailed Furty with a gaze that would split an atom, and then ran after her whining pet.

"What happened to you, Furty?" asked Benny. "We used to be friends."

For a long moment, Furty's gaze lost its focus, drifting out over Benny's shoulder.

"We used to hang out on the salthouse, remember?"

Furty didn't answer; it was as though his eyes were looking out but seeing in.

If Benny had shut up right there, he could have averted the events of the next few weeks, but he had to go and spoil it all with his big stupid gob. "What happened to you in that reform place, anyway?"

And bam, Furty was back, shaking his head as though Benny's comment had hit him like a slap. His eyes zoomed and whirred, closing in on the undaunted Wexford boy before him.

"I'll tell you what happened to me, Shaw. I wised up. I learned that no one is your friend. So from now on, I'm looking out for number one."

Benny hunted for a smart reply, but nothing came. "Look, Furty," he said, "we didn't know that trap was yours. Let's just forget about it and start over."

Furty shook his head ruefully. "Sorry, Shaw. Not possible. Another thing I learned in reform school was never forgive or forget. People take advantage."

Benny was getting a bit peeved with all this melodrama. "What did you do for the year? Read gangster books or something? Just do something or go home."

This would have been very impressive if a little warble hadn't crept into Benny's voice at the very last word.

"Oh don't worry, Benny. I'm planning already." Furty lifted himself from the bollard and brushed off the seat of his pants. "'Night, Shaw," he said loudly. "Good to see you again." He winked broadly. "For your Granda's benefit."

Benny returned the wink with his most insincere grin, but his stomach wasn't as cocky as his face. It churned noisily with nervous acids. "See you around, Furty boy."

Furty strolled up the quay, his words floating back ominously over his shoulder. "Count on it, Bernard lad. Count on it."

Benny sighed. It wasn't as though Furty was huge or anything. He'd had bigger fellows than that looking to separate his head from his shoulders. There was just something about the whole reform-school thing. Something that went beyond your usual teenage high jinks. They'd have to be on the lookout for him, no doubt about it.

Babe climbed over the stile, with murder, or at the very least dismemberment, on her mind. Conger was cradled in her arms, smiling a blissful doggy smile.

"Where is he?"

"Gone."

"Do you think we'll see him again?"

Benny plucked the words out of the air. "Count on it."

It'd be easy enough to introduce Furty as the baddie and leave it there. That wouldn't be altogether fair, though, because nobody is born nasty. Something happens to mold a person one way or the other. Sometimes it's a big thing—it wraps itself around your brain and shapes it accordingly. But usually it's everyday events that tap away on the mind until they've sculpted a new personality. These everyday events are called parents.

Furty was unlucky. He got the big earth-shattering event and the little ones too. It all went back to his mother and father. Whatever else goes wrong in a child's life, he'll more than likely pull through, if his parents are behind him. Well, Furty's parents weren't behind him, or in front of him, or anywhere else in the vicinity for that matter.

You couldn't blame his mother, she died when he was only nine. One Friday afternoon, little Furty came home from the sports day, two gold medals clutched in his grimy paws, to find the front yard full of people. Everyone was shaking their heads, and some of the women were sobbing into pieces of tissue. Furty thought something sad must have happened on *Coronation Street*—that was what usually had the women bawling.

So he ran into the house, waving the medals over his

head. And there was his Mammy, with the priest and the sergeant leaning over her. Furty knew immediately that his Mammy wasn't asleep, because she wasn't doing her little singsong snore. And you didn't generally get the priest and sergeant coming around to watch someone sleeping.

A terrible accident, they told him later. The tip of a thorn from a garden rose had worked its way from her thumb up along the arteries to her brain. Chance in a million, the doctor said.

It became his father's catchphrase whenever misfortune struck. *Chance in a million*, he'd snarl at a flat tire. *Chance in a million*, he'd rage at the losing horse he'd put his last fiver on. He said it as though he were cursed. Little Furty got the feeling that it was all his fault somehow.

So you had Jonjo Howlin and Furty on their own in the workman's cottage. Things were okay for a while, with Daddy doing his best to look out for his little boy. But he soon realized that Furty was well able to look after himself in most respects. He could wash and iron and make a better meal at a fry-up than Jonjo ever could. There was no harm in leaving a boy like that on his own. And if the young lad decided not to go to school the odd day, what about it? What use were Irish and poetry to a fisherman, anyway?

So, gradually, Furty became his own master. Cooking, cleaning, and making some decisions he probably wouldn't have made had there been a steady hand to guide him. Jonjo's hand was far from steady; free from the sobering influence of his wife, it was generally shaking with the aftereffects of drink, along with the rest of his body.

Furty was probably better off in the early days. He knew enough to keep himself fed and clean, and his cohorts were all harmless enough. The most trouble Paudie, young Benny, and the other boys got into was the odd spate of orchard robbing.

But when Furty landed in the regional secondary, he began hanging around with a bad crowd. The first time the police dropped him home for shoplifting, Jonjo battered him black and blue. But after that he didn't bother. You're your own man now, Furty, he'd say. Just be ready to pay the piper.

The piper's bill arrived two weeks after Furty's sixteenth birthday. A date marked in red ink on the police calendar. Furty and his cohorts decided to investigate the interior of a chip van left parked beside a local beach. Unfortunately for Furty, the van's owner happened to be asleep in the cab at the time. On hearing someone jimmying the skylight, he turned the ignition and sped off to the nearest police station. Imagine the policemen's delight when they found Furty still jammed in the skylight! Every man on duty came out for a look, before eventually prying free the offending teenager.

The judge gleefully sentenced him to a year in Saint Julian's, and that was when Furty discovered that he had no friends. In the nine months he actually served, no one came to visit. Not his father, not one of his so-called buddies, and certainly none of the old village friends that he'd spurned over the past few years.

For the first six months, the bitterness inside Furty festered. He sat and allocated blame to whoever he could think of. His mother for dying, his father for virtually abandoning him, and his teachers for branding him a troublemaker.

Then, his anger spent, Furty began to consider his own part in things. He was far from stupid, and had to admit that no one had forced him to climb on to the roof of the chip van. Furty felt the weight of responsibility bearing down on him.

Furty began to picture a new life for himself upon his release. He would get a job on the trawlers in Duncade. He'd start caring for his father, and re-establish contact with his old friends. No more shoplifting or joy riding. And certainly no more breaking and entering. Decision made, a weight lifted off Furty's shoulders. He became the person that he wanted to be. For once, rehabilitation actually seemed to be working. Then he was released.

With the best will in the world, Furty set about reassembling the pieces of his life. But things did not progress as he'd imagined on those lonely nights in Julian's. It was as though he had a sign around his neck saying "criminal." He couldn't get a job picking spuds, never mind working on the boats. His Da had gone over the edge altogether with the drink, stopping only to sleep. He was moody and insulting, wanting no part of his son's disgrace. Furty was certain his father would have taken a swing at him, if he hadn't sprouted over the last few months.

Because he was living at home, Furty wasn't eligible for the dole. So there was only one way for him to make a few bob. Lure hunting. It pained Furty to stoop to this, an occupation usually left to nippers and girls. But times were tough, and he did know the coast like the back of his hand. So you can imagine his disgust to find his bait trap cut adrift. He was livid. It was the last straw. Now they were trying to take the coastline from him. No, he decided. Enough was enough. It would have to be done cleverly, but one way or another those two blow-ins were going to be taught a lesson.

5

BAIT WARS

Benny was waiting by the gate the following morning. There were two reasons for this. One, he wanted to avoid another Happy Bunny episode. And two, he was excited because Da would be down for the weekend. When Pat Shaw arrived in Duncade, he felt so guilty about leaving his family for the week that he spoiled everybody rotten. Benny, being Benny, exploited this to the hilt.

Conger came belting around the corner, his claws skidding on the driveway gravel.

"Here, boy!" said Benny, expecting the usual snarl of disdain. But no! Conger skittered over and danced around the boy's ankles.

Benny laughed delightedly. "Good boy!" He sank to his knees, forgetting they were mortal enemies, and began tickling the dog's chin.

"You two made up, have ye?" Babe was sauntering toward them, wearing her usual uniform of baggy jeans, loose sweatshirt, and woolly hat.

"Well, we've enough to be worried about with Furty. I need all the friends I can get."

Babe nodded. "I suppose. What's the story with that chap, anyway?"

"I'm not sure," replied Benny. "I heard he beat up a chip van owner with a bit of frozen cod."

"You're not serious?"

"That's what I heard."

Babe hung her head forward so a mop of curly hair covered her face. "Thanks for standing up for me last night."

"What?" stammered Benny. "Well, you know, partners and all."

"Still, I'd rather be a girl than twice the man Furty Howlin is."

Benny's blush deepened. "Is that what I said?"

"Afraid so."

"You know what I meant. That you weren't just a girl . . ."

"Really?"

"Not that there's anything wrong with being a girl. It's just that normal girls don't do the stuff you do, they just like being pretty and stuff. . . ."

Babe swept back her hair, and for a moment Benny caught sight of her eyes. They were wide and brown.

"Benny," she said firmly.

"Yes?"

"Shut up."

"Okay. Yes. That would seem to be the best course of action. . . ."

"BENNY!"

"What? Oh, shut up. Right."

The rocks had been picked clean. For two hours Benny and Babe scoured every tide pool and weed field, finding only a few measly leads. Initially, Benny assumed that he was having yet another off day, but then he noticed Babe muttering darkly to herself, and he realized that he wasn't the only one coming up empty. They sat overlooking Black Chan, their meager catch spread on the grass before them.

"Three homemades!" said Babe, shaking her head incredulously. "Even in the middle of winter you'd do better than that. What in the name of God is going on?"

Benny squinted into the morning sun. He knew what his old hurling coach, Father Barty, would say. "We weren't first to the ball."

"What?"

"Someone beat us to it. Any guesses?"

Babe slapped her forehead. "Of course. That pirate Howlin. He must have been up at the crack of dawn."

Benny nodded, mightily relieved that he hadn't delayed them by sleeping in. "Yep. Must have been."

Conger growled, feeding off their frustration.

"We were here first," shouted Babe. "This is our stretch. He has all the way from here to Hook Head to search, but no, he has to pick this particular spot."

"Maybe we should move," suggested Benny meekly.

Babe shook her head emphatically. "No! No way! I spent six months learning these rocks. The whole summer would be gone before we'd start making money from another area! I'm not shifting!"

Benny raised his hands in surrender. "Okay, okay. I was only saying."

"Sorry," Babe sighed. "It's just that we were off to such a good start. Twenty-six pounds last night, you know."

Benny nearly choked. "How much?"

"Yep. Not bad, is it?"

Benny shook his head. Somehow he'd forgotten all about the money. Babe handed him a bank bag full of coins.

"There you go. Your first and last decent payday. There's no point setting up shop tonight with three leads."

Benny felt the weight of the money in his palm. "Now, pixie. Don't be so hasty."

"Sure, what chance have we?" muttered Babe dejectedly. "That chap must know every crack in the rocks around here."

"Ah now! Don't give up so easily there, young one. There's ways and means."

Babe kicked a sod of clay into the Chan. "Like what, for example?"

As usual, when he was trying to think, Benny had to put things in a hurling framework. "Well, if you look at this as half time. We're a few points behind going into the dressing room, so now we have to change the tactics. I think our basic strategy is sound, it's just our timing that's off."

"You don't speak English, I suppose?"

"Furty is beating us to the lures, simple as that."

"So all we have to do is . . ."

"Get here before him."

Babe started paying attention. "Your man is probably out here at the stroke of low tide. So if we come out an hour earlier, then we still have most of the rocks to search before that pirate drags his lazy backside out of bed."

"Exactly," grinned Benny.

The partners smiled broadly at each other, united by their plan, forgetting the culchie-townie grudge for a moment. Forgetting that beneath all the posing and smart comments, they were just a boy and a girl.

Furty lay on the salthouse smoking one of the cigarettes he'd lifted from his old man's pocket. A tupperware box full of lures sat up on a tuft of grass beside him. He twisted the ring on his old brass binoculars, focusing on the lip of

Black Chan. Two diminutive figures were sitting at the edge, heads hanging despondently. A mongrel mutt skipped around them, looking for attention. Furty chuckled to himself. "Did you like that one, Shaw? Did you like the few leads I left you?"

He lay back on the roof and blew a pillar of smoke at the sky. It was nice, Furty decided, being able to see the sky all day. All night too, if he felt like it. It'd be nicer though, he conceded, to have a few of the lads up here with him. Paudie and the boys, even the townie Shaw, messing and tussling like the old days. Furty growled, annoyed with himself. The old days were gone. Everyone had deserted him. The world had moved on while he was locked up in that hellhole.

Look out for number one, that was the only rule worth remembering. That, and maybe, don't get caught. The chip van, Furty decided, was stupid. He'd wasted nine months of his life out of pure stupidity. He wouldn't be that stupid again. No. If Shaw and that girl messed with him, there wouldn't be one shred of proof that he was involved with whatever misfortune befell them.

Benny and George had their faces pressed to the top-level window. From this vantage point they had a clear view of the whole promontory. Of course, they would have had a much better view from the balcony. But Jessica Shaw did not trust her offspring unsupervised at any height over four feet. She was trying to get an impressive dinner ready, and Granda was down at the dock sneering at the sub aqua club's dinghy. So the two boys would have to make do with an inside window.

Half past six now—Da should come tearing up the coast road at any moment. They jostled for space at the lighthouse's slit window.

"Budge over will you, Crawler!"

"I will not give an inch / even if you pinch."

"Hah!" Benny crowed triumphantly. "That's a forced rhyme! I heard Ma going on about that. Inch, pinch. Sure what's pinching got to do with anything? You just threw it in there to rhyme with inch. Call yourself a poet? Pathetic."

George was disgusted. He never would have used a weak rhyme like that in front of his mother, but he didn't think Benny, the philistine, would ever pick up on it. Truth be told, Georgie was getting a bit fed up of the whole rhyming thing, but he couldn't back down until ordered to by his parents. He reckoned Benny would crack in another couple of days, and he'd be instructed to desist, for peace's sake. Georgie was saved further embarrassment by the sight of a blue station wagon motoring along the narrow road. Benny did a quick check with his telescope, and was gone like a bullet.

"Ma!" he roared. "Ma! Da's here!"

One hand on the brass bannister, he went belting off

down the spiral staircase, centrifugal force nearly tearing his arm out of its socket. Georgie followed tentatively, stepping carefully as though each step would suddenly become a cliff face.

If Georgie was his mother's son, then Benny was his father's boy. Two sports fanatics, with low tolerance for things artistic—it nearly scared Jessica Shaw how alike they were. Right down to the fishhook cowlicks on the crowns of their heads. She'd tried, God knows, to inject some culture through their leathery hides, but each attempt inevitably culminated in mortification for herself. The most notable occasions being when Bernard asked a world-famous abstract artist was he not able to paint proper? And Pat Shaw nodding off during Swan Lake and whacking his head on the balcony rail. Jessica shuddered at the memory. By the time she reached the lighthouse door, Pat and Benny were already rolling around on the lawn in a mock tussle.

Every time Pat and Jessie were reunited, it was like one of those slow motion movies. They caught sight of each other, then smiled and hugged for several moments. It made Benny want to barf. All this lovey-dovey bit was for young people, not parents.

"Come on, come on!" he said trying to insert himself between his parents. "There are minors present, you know."

They disentangled reluctantly, Jessie tucking a red curl

behind her ear. Pat was blushing like a kid on a date. He turned to his sons.

"Well, lads? Have a good week?"

Georgie got his speak in first. "He did grievous bodily harm / to my arm."

Pat groaned. Complaints already. And poetry. Benny jumped to his own defence.

"Hang on there now, Craw . . . Georgie boy. I already got punished for that. Anyway, he was rhyming, and he threatened to break my hurley."

Da gasped. "What?"

Georgie shrugged. "Just a threat." He glanced slyly at Benny. "Didn't do it . . . yet."

Pat raised his hands. "All right, the pair of you! Give it a rest, for God's sake!"

He gave his sons his best stern stare. "Now, here's the way it is. Benny, you are never to hit your brother, under any circumstances. And you, George, are to stay away from Benny's hurley, and give up that rhyming. You're driving me mental."

"But, Daddy," moaned George. "I'm trying to be creative."

"I know what you're trying to do," said Pat pointedly. "Listen, George boy. If you feel a rhyme coming on, scribble it down on your pad, and I'll set by a special time to listen to all your efforts. We'll all listen."

"Sort of like a show?"

"Exactly."

"All, Da?"

Pat levelled his gaze at Benny. "We'll all listen, and we'll like it, or I might have to reconsider this junior disco you've been begging me to go to."

Benny opened his mouth to object, but the go-on-I-dare-you look on his father's face changed his mind for him.

Jessica linked her husband. "Such dazzling negotiation skills. I'm impressed."

"Maybe now we can enjoy the weekend."

Jessica ruffled her eldest's hair. "Guess what? Benny's found himself a little girlfriend."

Benny bristled. "I have not!"

Pat laughed. "Go on, Benny!"

Benny struggled to maintain his scowl. "She's my business partner!"

"She's Babe," added Jessica.

"A babe! Good man!"

Jessica elbowed him in the ribs. "Babe, you pig. Her name is Babe!"

"Oh, right."

Jessica shook her head in despair. Where, oh where, were all the so-called new men? There were none in Duncade, that was for sure.

Happy Bunny was just congratulating Benny on his contributions to world peace, when real life broke through. It was still nighttime, pitch black except for the swing of the beam every five seconds. So what was he doing awake? In the momentary glow of the lighthouse beam, Benny saw a blue dot glowing spookily by the door. The pinhole illumination could nearly have been Conger's voodoo eye if it hadn't been floating five feet off the ground. The bedroom light flicked on. Benny clamped his eyes shut against the sudden glare, afraid to open them again in case what he thought he saw was still there.

Someone cleared their throat. It was Da. Benny had been distracted from mischief-making too often by that sound not to recognize it. Reluctantly, Benny opened his eyes. He groaned. The vision was still there. Da was standing at the door in his pajamas. He had Conger in one fist, Babe in the other and an extremely peeved look on his face.

Pat Shaw raised an eyebrow. "Benny?"

"I've never met that person before in my life. I don't know the mutt either."

"Benny?"

"Oh, all right," Benny sighed. "It's Babe, you know, my . . ."

"Girlfriend?"

"Partner," spluttered Babe indignantly.

"I see. And is it your business practice to sneak into other people's houses in the middle of the night, young lady?"

"The Captain said it was all right."

Da sighed. "I'll bet he did too. You're lucky I didn't skull the pair of you for burglars."

You could see Babe's mind working, deciding whether or not to respond to this warning. Benny shook his head gently. They were in enough trouble already.

"Right, Benny. Get dressed. Babe here will be waiting outside."

"Okay, Dad."

"Righto, Mr. Shaw."

"Never mind your okays and your rightos, just don't let me catch you in this lighthouse after daylight hours." Da trained a nasty eye on Conger. "Because if I do, I'll be having a Korean sandwich."

Babe had no clue what that meant, but it sounded ominous.

Benny pulled on his jeans and jersey and stumbled down the spiral staircase. Babe was waiting by the gate, a rucksack slung over her shoulder.

"What's in a Korean sandwich, townie?"

"Dunno," replied Benny, rubbing sleep from his eyes. "Koreans, I suppose."

He looked at the sky; a band of pale red was creeping up from the horizon. "What time is it, anyway?"

"About quarter to five, I suppose."

"Quarter to what?"

"It was your idea, Benny. First to the ball, you said."

Benny scowled. "Okay then, I suppose. What's in the bag?"

Babe swung the knapsack on to the wall and opened the drawstring. "Some extra equipment I rigged up." She pulled out two bicycle lamps with elastic straps dangling from the clasps. "These go on your head, see, like a miner's light."

Benny was impressed. "Good thinking, pixie. Did the fairy king tell you that one?" He pulled the elastic around his skull and switched on. "I hope no one thinks we're the lighthouse."

Babe sniggered. "Who'd be that stupid . . ." She paused.

"Don't say it."

"Except maybe townies."

"I knew you were going to say that! When are you going to give the townie thing a rest?"

"Whenever you lay off the pixie bit."

"Never, then."

"Okay by me . . . Oh, and Benny?"

"What?"

"I got the elastic for your lamp from one of me Dad's old underpants."

Benny tore the lamp off his head. "You didn't, did you?"

Babe shrugged. "Might have."

"Come on now, Babe. That's not funny."

"I think it's hilarious."

"Swap then."

"No way, townie. I don't want your fleas."

"I don't have fleas, pixie!"

"Oh, they must be lice so."

Benny felt a headache coming on. He wasn't used to this level of banter before breakfast.

Even in the dark, they could tell the tide was out. The stink of uncovered weed, diesel fuel, and rotting fish rose up out of the dock like a rancid fog. Without sunlight it was easy to imagine the smell reaching out smoky tendrils to curl up your nose.

Clipper was dragging a punt over to the short wall, tired out from a night in the deep-sea cod grounds.

"Any luck, Clipper?" Babe shouted down to him.

Clipper pulled a sackcloth from the top of a bait box. A few dozen sandy cod lay inside, their beards still twitching. "Want to earn a pound each?" he called up to them.

Benny got an I-just-swallowed-a-live-worm feeling in his stomach.

Babe glanced at her watch. "'Course we do. We've got a few minutes."

"Good. Good. Here, take the box."

Clipper balanced on the keel of the grounded punt and passed up the plastic box. Suffocating fish slithered and flapped weakly, heaping in the lower end.

"What do we have to do?" asked Benny, horribly afraid he already knew the answer.

Babe grinned, pulling her scaling knife from its sheath. "Gut the lot of 'em," she said. "That's not a problem for you, is it, townie?"

"No," croaked Benny weakly. "I've done it before, hundreds of times."

This, of course, wasn't strictly true. Actually, it was a big fat lie. But Bernard Shaw was hardly going to admit to a girl that he had spent the last eight summers avoiding having to gut fish.

"Great stuff. You're a veteran so. Should only take us five minutes between us."

They hauled the jittering box over to the slip and set it at the water's edge. The morning sun crested the horizon, dabbing crimson flecks on the harbor wavelets. The beauty was lost on Benny. He was more concerned with having to plunge his hands into a fish's innards.

"So, anyway," he said casually, "which method do you prefer?"

Babe selected the biggest fish in the box. A fat ten-pounder, at least two feet in length.

"Well," she said, dragging the unfortunate fish by the gills onto the flat stone. "Personally I like to lop off the head first, then go down the neck hole to the tailbone."

She demonstrated, slicing the cod's head off with three strong strokes of her knife. The backbone held out for a second then snapped under the pressure of the jagged blade. Benny would nearly swear that the disembodied head was staring at the rest of itself, wondering what was going on. Babe slid her Leatherman down the inside of the fish's pale belly and flicked outward. The fleshy meat flopped apart in two flaps and the stringy balloons of intestines bulged out. Babe scooped the guts into her hand and tore them away from the vertebrae.

"That's the quickest way," she said, firing the slimy mass into the water. A gaggle of beady-eyed seagulls converged on the morsels. With cruelly hooked yellow beaks they rent the veiny feast apart.

Benny paled. "Yep, that's the way I do it too."

"Right so," muttered Babe, bending to the task. "Let's get a shift on, and get up the rocks before Furty shows up."

Benny selected a fish. A little guy that looked stone dead. 'Course, as soon as he laid it on the slabs, the poor chap began flapping its tail and flaring its gills trying to suck some oxygen out of the air. Benny pulled his knife from its homemade sheath. Still a bit short on funds, it was a kitchen knife rather than a proper scaler.

He swallowed and cut into the cod's neck. The fish went mad for a second, as you would, then went limp. Before it gave up the ghost, the fish's last act was to squirt a stream of brown goo all over Benny's jersey.

Babe laughed. "Always point the backside away from you, townie."

"What?" groaned Benny. "You mean that's . . ."

"Yep."

"Oh no!"

After that indignity, Benny had no more sympathy for that particular fish. He completed the task quickly and flung the guts into the dock. A strange sense of pride came over him. Doubtless something to do with the hunter's instinct. His hands were covered with blood, slime, and strands of meat. It wasn't that bad at all. He picked his second victim, a big boy this time.

Clipper opened up each fish, examining the pair's handiwork.

"All right, I suppose," he admitted. "What was it? Fifty pence each?"

Benny laughed. "Good one, Clipper. Hand over the cash before we stuff the guts back in."

Clipper undid the clasps of his oilskins. "Listen, lads, I haven't a penny on me. I'll see ye by the bench later. Okay?"

Babe nodded. "That's perfect, Clipper boy. There's no shops over the bank anyway."

Clipper yawned, the action cracking the mask of scales on his face. "Right so. I'm off for a nap." He winked at Benny. "I wish I had a nice soft girl's job like yer Granda. And you can tell him I said that too." Laughing, he shuffled over to the fresh-water pump and began rinsing his gear.

The sky was lightening considerably. The sun was a hemisphere now, rising out of a calm sea.

"Right, pixie," said Benny. "Come on and let's get this done. I'm starving already."

The partners climbed through the Norman arch and began their search at the Babby's Pool. Conger pawed the rock pools, trying to catch the quicksilver shrimps. He thrust his nose into the tendrils of exposed sea anemones, rearing back when they quivered into life. Being the stupid mutt that he was, Conger was genuinely surprised every time this happened.

They strapped on the lamps, Benny feeling slightly sheepish at the thoughts of the elastic's origins. But he couldn't deny their effectiveness. The night had not yet retreated, and what light there was could not penetrate the lee of the limestone shelves.

Their new strategy was rewarded almost immediately, Benny's beam picked out a sliver of metal nestling in a hank of dulse.

"Bingo!" he exclaimed, reaching in to claim the bait, and for once he didn't even snag his fingers. It was a jumbo German. Fresh in the water too, not a spot of rust on it. Just a green weed smear. That would come off with a rub of spirits.

Babe smiled. "First blood to us. I've a feeling this is going to be a good day."

Babe was right. The rocks yielded a bumper harvest of lures. Even under the rising sun, the lamps picked out dark corners that had never before been investigated. They found lures that had been shrouded in darkness for years. Some were rusted to mere stalks, while others were salvageable with a new hook and some cosmetic surgery.

They stopped to take inventory at Horatio's Bridge. Only halfway to the Chan and already Babe's pack was swelling with their finds.

"Furty Howlin!" said Babe disdainfully. "Where does someone get a name like Furty, anyway? In a joke shop?"

An old proverb about glass houses and stones came into Benny's mind, but he kept it to himself.

"Furt is a footballing term," he explained. "A furt is when some cul . . . some person can't kick a ball properly and just bogs it up the field with his big toe. Good for distance, bad for accuracy. I'd say our boy must've made a name for himself as a bogman footballer in his younger days."

"So, what's his real name then?"

Benny shrugged. "I dunno. Probably Patsy or Mickser or some other wooller's name. I can't understand it. There's millions of you culchies, and you all use the same four names. No wonder everyone has a nickname."

Babe sniggered. "I wish we had creative mothers like yours, Ber-nard."

Benny laughed. "Oh ha ha, most humorous, pixie."

This was actually a momentous occurrence. For the first time in Benny Shaw's short life, he had actually laughed at himself. It had happened naturally, just sort of slipped by him. And it had a lot to do with his partner. It was just hard to take offense from Babe. There was something about her. Maybe it was the fact that if you were upset by all her insults, you'd be whining all day.

"So, what have we got?"

Babe spread the lures out on the rocks. "Two Germans, one jumbo, thanks to you. Four spooners, two perfect. Five Vee Bees, none to be given away."

"Don't worry, I've learned my lesson."

"And one red-eye, as sold to Anto the other day."

"Not bad," said Benny.

"And we still have a good way to go."

The sun was up now, boiling the morning gauze of cloud from the sky. A Mediterranean blue poked through the widening holes. It was going to be a scorcher. They kept their lights on anyway, leaning low to the ground, poking their heads under flat rock shelves and into dank fissures.

It was punishing work, their clothes damp and steaming, their shoulders sore from sun and strain. But every time they spied the gleam of metal in the grip of tangleweed or trapped in the stone fingers of eroded limestone, the struggle became worthwhile. Benny was especially determined. He was holding his own today, and he knew it.

A question he'd been meaning to ask was answered on Frenchy's Peak. As the searchers crawled to the water's edge, Conger continued to investigate the rock pools. Suddenly he began to growl menacingly, hackles rising like blades through his fur.

"What's wrong with him?" asked Benny.

Babe straightened, glancing over at her pet.

"Get away from there!" she commanded immediately, lurching stiffly to her feet. Benny ran to join her beside the pool. Conger was staring into the shadowy depths, his eyes flitting around after some elusive shadow.

"Granda told me about this pool," commented Benny.

"Not now, townie," moaned Babe.

"No, no. This is interesting. Apparently this particular pool is linked to the sea by an underground tunnel. Granda says that all sorts of yokes swim up the channel and can't get back out. A shark got in here in the fifties.

Took the leg off some young fellow going for a paddle. But what they usually get is—"

"Conger eels," interrupted Babe.

"Yes, but how did you . . ."

It was hard to say if the dog went for the eel, or the eel attacked the dog. Either way, there was a writhing mass of flesh and teeth thrashing on the rock before Benny knew what was going on.

Babe grabbed his arm. "On the rocks! Get up on the rocks!"

Benny jumped up on to the nearest shelf, narrowly avoiding the eel's tail. They watched with helpless fascination as canine and fish fought it out. It was a strange battle. The dog had maneuverability, but the eel had the strength and the teeth. Four foot of slick black aggression, with a row of razors at the end of it. The conger thrashed wildly, gnashing his jaws ceaselessly. It was an awesome sight. Benny was fully aware that if those jaws clamped on bone, just once, then the fight was over. He took a moment to glance at Babe. She, too, was aware of the danger her pet was in.

Conger pranced in and out of the eel's reach, goading him. Babe called him to heel, but the usually obedient animal was having none of it. Conger had, for the duration of this confrontation, lost any shred of domesticity that his mistress had instilled in him.

Suddenly the dog pounced. He saw an opening and went for it. In a flash, his jaws were clamped around the eel's throat. The eel's teeth were useless, so it employed the only other weapon available to it. A ripple passed along its length, and suddenly two meaty coils were wrapped around the dog's body. It was a question of stamina now. The dog bit deep, draining the life's blood from its adversary, while the conger squeezed with the desperation of the dying.

For a long minute the struggle continued, then suddenly the coils relaxed, unraveling on the rocks. Conger gave the throat one last shake to be sure, and then collapsed from exhaustion.

Babe rushed to her dog's side. "You stupid animal!" she shouted, checking every inch of fur for puncture marks.

Benny did not hop down from his perch quite so quickly. "You sure that thing's dead?"

Babe glanced at the eel. "Certain. Congers never give up while they've a breath of life in them. Pick that fellow up and we'll sell him to Clipper for lobster bait."

Benny poked the corpse with his toe. "I dunno. It's an awfully mean-looking corpse." He leaned down staring into the conger's eye. It seemed to stare back at him, a flat glittering disk. He reached out a hand to pick up the eel, when Conger roused himself and squatted on the dead fish.

"Fair enough," said Benny. "You earned it."

Babe wiped a sheen of sweat from her forehead, some of the color returning to her face. "That dog'll give me a heart attack yet," she declared.

Benny nodded. "Well, at least now I don't have to ask why you named him Conger."

"He used to be called Eejit. But it was changed by popular demand when he trotted up the dock with an eel in his gob."

Benny watched the mutt tormenting the dead eel. "I don't know. I think Eejit kind of suits him."

By the time they were heading back across the meadows, they had at least twenty saleable lures. More than enough to set up shop that night. Benny was tired, stiff, and stinking of fish scales and worse. But he felt great. The cuts and scrapes that he would once have gone whining to Ma about, he now regarded as badges of hard labor.

They strolled through the long grass, chatting affably for once. Conger amused himself by chasing the odd sheep they encountered. The sheep weren't that worried, though. They seemed to sense that Conger would never relinquish the eel in his mouth long enough to bite them.

They collided with Furty at the stile. It was six fifteen, the stroke of low tide. It was a situation you couldn't ignore. Three people and only room for one to get by. A

Trojans-at-the-pass sort of thing. For an instant, surprise flitted across Furty's face, then he was stony again.

"Doing a bit of mining, girls?"

Benny's hand shot to the lamp which sat, forgotten, on his forehead. "Listen, Furty," he began. "It's just hitting low tide now. There's loads of rock that we didn't search."

"Search!" snorted Furty. "Searching is for kids like yourselves. I'm setting a new trap today." He patted a hank of net over his shoulder. "I'm putting this down at Frenchy's Peak, and God help the unfortunate blow-in that lays a finger on it."

"Pirate," muttered Babe.

Furty glared at her. "Being a girl won't protect you forever. I may not be able to hit you, but I could certainly leave a poisoned steak outside your door some morning."

Babe paled. "You . . . You . . ."

Before she could formulate a response, Furty brushed past, whistling merrily: "How Much Is That Doggy in the Window?"

Benny stared after him, aghast that someone he'd once considered a friend could have changed so much.

6

DISCO KING

The inquisition was in session. Benny sat at the kitchen table flanked by the family elders.

"So," said Da. "Tell me about this disco thing again."

Benny sighed mightily. "We've been through this a million times."

Da's eyes narrowed. "And we'll go through it a million more until we're satisfied."

"Ah, Da!"

"Fine. Forget it altogether. Don't go."

Jessica put a hand on her husband's arm. "Pat. Take it easy."

Benny knew the tactics. He'd seen it on telly. Good cop, bad cop. But with Granda there, it was good cop, bad cop, and smart aleck cop. It was a ritual they put him through every single time he wanted to go somewhere. You'd swear he was going to get into trouble or something. Benny adjusted his expression to angelic.

"Ah here!" Pat said. "Look at the face on him. I never trust Benny when he puts on the innocent act."

"What face?" protested Benny.

"There's something you're not telling me!"

"Like what?"

"Now, that's a stupid question, isn't it? How am I supposed to know what you're not telling me?"

Georgie winced. He had a vested interest in this conversation and Benny was blowing it.

Da took a deep breath. "Right so. From the top."

Benny resisted the urge to ask for his attorney.

"What exactly is it?"

"A junior disco."

"Where?"

"Ah, Da! I told you all—"

"Where?"

Benny sighed mightily. "Saint Brigid's hall. Which is in Newford, by the way, in case you're wondering."

Da smiled thinly. "Oh yes, Bernard. This is an excellent time to use sarcasm. Good choice."

Benny frowned. He suspected Da himself was using sarcasm, but he wasn't sure.

Ma tried to get the interrogation back on track. "What time, Bernard?"

"Seven to ten."

"Ten? That's awfully late."

Benny balked. "Late? I'm thirteen now, Ma . . . Mam."

"Physically maybe. I don't know about mentally."

"Are you saying I'm immature?"

"Well . . ."

"I am not immature. I am not!"

The Shaw parents gave each other knowing looks.

"You see, this is what we mean, Bernard. Listen to yourself. You can't even talk to your own parents without throwing a fit."

Benny took a deep shuddering breath. "I am not throwing a fit," he said with exceptional calmness. "I just think it's unfair how you're putting me on trial over something that's a natural part of my development. I can't stay a baby forever."

It was a good point, well stated. He could see that he'd made a dent in the armor. That shook you, he thought. Total rubbish, of course, but effective all the same.

Jessica twisted a strand of red hair. "Well, of course we want you to grow up, Bernard. It's just that we can't help worrying about you. It's because we love you."

Benny smiled understandingly. "I know, Mam. But you don't have to worry. There's a whole crowd of us going. We'll all cycle together, and there's a couple of priests in charge."

Da tried a last-ditch attempt. "Did you check your brakes?"

"Yes, Da."

"Have you got a puncture kit?"

"Yes, Da."

"Clean underwear?" Granda broke down, sniggering at his own wittiness.

"Paddy!" spluttered Jessica, trying to contain a smile.

Even Da had to grin. Maybe he was being a bit protective.

"Okay, so. We'll call it a trial run. If you're back one second after ten forty-five, then that's your discos over for the summer."

"Yes, Da," said Benny humbly.

Da squinted at him. "Don't!"

"I'm not!"

"Well, don't!"

Georgie was waiting out by the fuel shed. "I told you," he said.

Benny smiled at his little brother. Another first. "I have to admit it, young lad. It was the natural-part-of-my-development bit that swung it."

"And?"

Benny dug fifty pence out of his pocket and flicked it to Georgie. "Good idea—worth every penny."

George, being George, missed the tossed coin and had to go chasing down the driveway after it. Benny sighed. Ah well, at least his brother had brains.

The convoy swung by at half past five. These were the cycling equivalents of Conger. A crowd of mongrels. Paudie was mounted on an ancient black high nelly, stripped down to the essentials. No mudguards, no lights, and, of course, no brakes. Brakes, apparently, were for girls. Seanie and Sean Ahern rode identical Triumph Twenties—even the rust patterns seemed similar. With those little wheels, these boys were going to have to do some pedaling to keep up. Babe, of course, arrived on the Rolls-Royce of mountain bikes. A rough rider twelve-speed, complete with elbow rests and water bottle.

Benny nodded at the bike. "Lures?" he asked.

"Yep," said Babe. "Summer before last."

Benny studied his culchie cohorts. They all seemed to be sporting a sort of disco uniform, including Babe. Baggy jeans, long shirt left hanging out, and big hiking boots. Babe had the obligatory woolly hat jammed over her forehead, too. Benny felt like a sore thumb in his sweatshirt and chinos. Still, too late to change now. He swung a leg over his five-speed racer.

"Are we going, then, or do I have to wait around for you farmers all day?"

Paudie laughed. "Shuddup now, townie, or I'll have to get Babe here to beat you up."

Babe swung a kick at the big farmer's leg. "The

137

townie's my partner. I can't be beating him up for anything less than two-fifty."

Their slagging was interrupted by Benny's parents striding down the drive.

"Hey, Benny," called Da. "What's the story?"

Benny, like most teenagers, did not appreciate his independence being challenged in front of his peers.

"We're going to the junior disco," he said through clenched teeth. "Remember?"

"I thought that didn't start until seven."

"It doesn't, Da. But it'll take half an hour to cycle in. Then we're going to get something to eat in Badger's Burgers."

"I've got a pound of fat in the fridge," said Jessica. "Why don't you just eat that?"

Benny struggled with his patience. This, he knew, was the final test. Make it through this without exploding, and he was on the way to his first disco.

"I'll get the vegetarian burger, then."

Da smiled, in spite of himself. Greasy burgers were not high on his fret list. "Okay then, Bosun. Ten forty-five, remember."

Jessica kissed her son on the cheek. "Take care now, Bernard."

"Will do, Mam. See you later."

The Shaw parents walked up the driveway reluctantly,

glancing back at their eldest as though he were going off to war.

Sean Ahern jumped off his bike. "Take care now, Bernard," he gushed, kissing Benny soundly on the cheek.

Benny felt this merited a bursting, and launched himself at the twin. They only stopped scuffling when they realized that the rest of the convoy had cycled off without them. Benny gave Sean one last dead leg and hopped on his bike. He slapped her into fifth, putting his weight on the pedals.

He could feel the excitement building in his stomach. His first disco. Benny wasn't sure what he was expecting. But it was bound to be different. Another step away from childhood. He couldn't wait.

The first stretch was the worst. Two miles of straight, flat road, with barely a bend or a bump to break the monotony. Away in the distance the gray rectangle of the parish church sat on the horizon, but no matter how hard you pedaled, it never seemed to get any closer. Locals referred to this stretch as "the road that killed the beggarman." According to Granda, some poor tramp had made it all the way from Malin Head, only to drop dead at the sight of this seemingly endless ribbon of tarmac. With the perspiration pasting the sweatshirt to his back, Benny could well believe it.

Benny and Babe were already relaxing by the church pump by the time the rest of them arrived. In the absence of brakes, Paudie stopped his machine by driving into the ditch and rolling on to the shoulder of the road. It was a risky method at best, and virtually guaranteed to destroy Paudie's clothes before he ever reached the disco.

They dismounted for a brief break, all thrusting their gobs under the pump in turn. The pump itself was an ancient mechanism, with a curved arm and lion's mouth for a spout. One person pumped, one drank. Mastering the flow was a delicate operation. Too slow and the water came out in an unsatisfying trickle, too fast and you drowned whoever's upturned face was gasping for a cool drink. So, obviously, the idea was to lure drinkers in with a steady flow, and then try to drench them with a sudden deluge.

Babe took a packet of Kimberley cookies from her bag, and stuck them in a ditch behind the pump. "For the way back."

"Good thinking, pixie," said Benny, shaking the water from his hair.

"Yep. We'll be glad of these at half past ten tonight."

Benny flattened his cowlick. "I wonder where Furty's at?"

Babe shrugged. "Well, he won't be at the junior disco, that's for sure. I suppose he's over on the rocks, trying to steal our customers."

"Let him go. He won't make a lot of friends with his temper."

"Maybe he can be sweet when he wants to be?"

"We'll find out tomorrow night, one way or the other."

Newford was what Anto might have called Yeehaw Heaven. A small fishing village on the southeast coast, it was a step up from Duncade in that it had two streets. In winter, Newford was the preserve of rural activity. Tractors rumbled down the main street, depositing muck from their monster tire treads. Young chaps on horses raced each other around the fields, and old men in suits sat on their front windowsills smoking filterless cigarettes.

But once the school holiday bell sounded, half of Dublin descended on the village's two caravan parks, and for eight weeks, Newford rang with the noise of children screaming, radios blaring, and boys and girls ignoring each other. And it's amazing how much noise people ignoring each other can make.

The Duncade posse swung into town, trying their best to look unconcerned and suave. This is not an easy feat when you've just cycled six miles, and salty sheets of sweat are blurring your vision, adding several pounds' weight to your clothing. So while Benny and company imagined themselves as mysterious and possibly lethal strangers, what they actually resembled was a crowd of mobile corpses that had just crawled out of a volcano.

They skidded to a halt outside Badger's Burgers, a local chip shop of dubious standards. It was always wise to bite tenderly into your burger, in case the center was still frozen. But the lure of Badger's was that it had video games down at the back, and Badger would let you hang about all day if you bought so much as a packet of ketchup.

The boys dismounted, and if there had been a post, they would have hitched their bikes to it. Paudie led the way, pulling a sheaf of fivers from his pocket. "How's the form there, Badger?"

Badger, a lanky character with a shock of red curly hair, grunted a greeting and then returned to picking a hair from a frying sausage. "Burgers and chips all 'round, is it?"

Benny nodded, though his stomach begged him to refuse. He couldn't. It was almost like a rite of passage.

"Right so, Badger," said Paudie. "That's five burgers and five chips so."

Badger grunted an affirmative.

"I'd like mine cooked, please," piped up Babe.

Badger glanced up sharply, tipping ash from his cigarette on to the grill. "Oh, a smart aleck, is it?"

"No," retorted Babe. "Just a health inspector."

Badger groaned. "Oh she's great, she is, Paudie. Why don't you bring her more often?"

"I would, but her little legs can't keep up."

"Shuddup you!"

"Temper! You've no dog to save you now."

Seanie grinned. "Sure, maybe her boyfriend will save her."

Benny chuckled away until he realized they were talking about him. "Seanie! I'm getting fed up beating you."

"Oh no!" cried Seanie. "It's Sir Townie come to save the maiden."

And things would probably have gone on like that—good-natured ribbing with a grain of truth in it—if it hadn't been for the arrival of a certain Furty Howlin.

"Would you look at who it is!" came his voice, laden with contempt.

Benny felt his stomach begin to churn, like some monkey was playing the bongos in there.

"Furty boy," Paudie greeted him, "how's the form with you?"

Furty grinned magnanimously. "Sure, not too bad, Paudie."

"How's the free world treating you?"

"Better than the other one."

Nervous laughter time. Nobody was comfortable with prison jokes.

Furty nodded toward Babe and partner. "So, when did you start hanging around with poachers?"

Paudie stiffened. "What?"

"Poachers. Those two blow-ins. Coming in here and searching my lure stretch."

"The rocks belong to whoever works them, Furty."

"What are you? Some sort of Red Indian or something? That's my stretch, and those two are only a pair of dirty poachers."

Badger straightened behind the counter. He was only a skinny fellow, but he had the wide-eyed look of a maniac.

"You see that, Furty?" he inquired pleasantly, holding up a steaming spatula.

Furty nodded.

"Well, I'll brand you like a brown-eyed calf if you don't stop your messing in my establishment."

Everyone was united in shock that Badger could refer to this hovel as an establishment. Still, with the blade of the spatula steaming through the grease, it was an effective threat. Badger reinforced the image by mashing the utensil into a burger. A spitting stream of fat and steam rose from the meat.

"Okay, Badger," said Furty. "Keep your hair on. This can wait. I've got all summer." He threw Benny one more poisonous glare and left the establishment.

"Five burgers, was it?" said Badger, the incident already forgotten. When you're dealing with caravaning Dubliners all season, you soon develop a thick skin.

Paudie took the proferred paper bag and hurried to a

table before it split. "I hope you two know what you're doing, messing with Furty."

"I hope so too," Benny muttered.

Paudie's usually blissful brow was wrinkled. "That chap is bad news. Bad news."

Babe took one bite of her burger and dumped it in the bin. "Never mind him. This is our night off, and we're going to enjoy it."

Benny nodded, unconvinced.

"Sure you might as well," said Seanie. "Furty's probably going to kill you tomorrow anyway."

Saint Brigid's hall looked like something out of an old black-and-white movie. Actually, it would have looked considerably better in a black-and-white movie because of the dreadful olive green paint slapped on the walls. It was one of your multipurpose village halls, used for basketball, Legion of Mary meetings, Farmers Giving Out About Politicians meetings, and, during the summer, junior discos. The only concessions made to the fact that there was a young people's dance going on that evening were a few limp balloons tacked up over the door, and two flashing orange lights, that Benny suspected had been lifted from the nearest road works.

They paid their two quid in and made straight for the snack bar. It was Lucozades all around.

Slurping away through a stripy straw, Benny scanned his first disco. Even though the music hadn't started yet, there was a fair crowd milling around the hall. It was easy spotting the Dublin crowd. The boys all had earrings, and the girls all had their bellies hanging out like junior Spice Girls. But no matter how cool they pretended to be, it was too early in the night for anyone to venture across the barren center of the hall. It was girls down one side, and boys down the other.

Benny elbowed Babe. "Hey. Shouldn't you be over there, pixie?"

Babe elbowed him back, a tad forcefully. "Why?"

"You know. Girls, boys, that sort of thing."

"What's your point, townie?"

"Well, you're a . . . you know—girl."

"Who are you calling . . ." began Babe, then stopped. "I know I'm a girl, eejit. I'm just not a girl-girl."

Benny nodded. "I understand perfectly."

Babe frowned. "And what do you mean by that?"

"Well, what you said. You're a girl, just not a girl-girl. Ribbons and giggling and all that."

"You are such a caveman, Bernard Shaw."

"Have you been talking to my mother?" asked Benny suspiciously.

"So you think I can't be a girl?"

"Hold on there now, partner. That's not what I said."

"Never mind the partner bit! I can be as good a girl as any man here. That's not what I . . . You know what I mean. God, Benny, you get me so annoyed!"

Benny was smart enough to realize that this had little to do with him. "Calm down there, Babe. I only said—"

"I'll show you, townie!"

"You don't have to show me anything!"

"We'll see about that!"

Babe stalked off to the bathroom, her rucksack bouncing with every step. Benny sighed. There went one angry pixie. So now Babe was going to try to be a proper girl. Babe! Dumpy, frumpy Babe Meara. This was going to be embarrassing.

Benny had to admit that this disco lark wasn't shaping up like he'd hoped. He wasn't sure what exactly he'd been expecting, but it certainly wasn't this! Benny had entertained vague visions of smiling trendy teenagers bopping away to the latest hits, with clouds of dry ice floating around their knees. And in the middle of it all would be Benny Shaw, having just discovered a natural talent for dancing. Girls would float by in slow motion, pausing only to admire the Wexford boy's skill as he gyrated under the strobe lights. Nice dream, shame about the reality.

In the real world, none of the boys had stirred off their seats in over half an hour. They sat chasing dribbles around the bottom of Lucozade bottles, staring enviously at the Dubliners who danced away without a hang-up in the world. They were really cool, too, with all these little flicks and hand movements like you'd see on "Top of the Pops."

Everything changed in an instant as soon as the heavy metal came on. Before the first bars of some Iron Maiden song had finished reverberating through his cranium, Benny found himself being dragged into the center of the hall. As if by magic, every Dub in the place disappeared from the dance floor. A large circle of locals began performing strange actions with their hands. It was as though they were tuning guitars. Guitars that they didn't have. Benny groaned. Oh God, no! Not air guitars.

It was quite impressive really. At the end of the first verse, fifty-odd teenagers twanged their invisible strings in perfect unison. It was a fantastic feat of choreography. They stomped and headbanged and sang the guitar chords rather than the words. Benny felt a primal excitement building in his gut. First his toe started, then his shoulders, and before he knew what was going on, he was headbanging with the best of them.

By the third song, Benny had lost the run of himself altogether. He'd decided that he was fed up with the air guitar, and decided to play the air drums instead. Initially this departure was viewed with some skepticism by the metal heads—similar to the reaction Columbus received on suggesting the world was round. But then the boys saw the possibilities. You could keep a nice steady beat for the verses, and then go into spasms for the solos. By the end of "Highway to Hell," half of the orchestra were banging invisible drums, and Benny was assured of a place in the metal circle for life.

Their tribal dance was cut short by a slow set. It was the Dubs' turn again. They oozed on to the floor, actually dancing with girls. Benny wasn't sure if he was envious or disgusted. A year ago he could have told you exactly what he thought about girls. But now he wasn't so sure. He was sure about one thing, though. There was no way in the world he was walking across the middle of that floor to have some young one turn up her nose at him. Benny rolled a Coke can along his forehead. Absolutely no way. He was just going to sit right here until the next heavy metal set.

Paudie slapped his knees. "Right, so. Wish me luck."

"Where are you going?"

"Well now, you hardly think I'm going to sit here with you planks while all those Dublin girls are just dying for me to give them a dance."

Benny's throat felt suddenly dry. "Suppose not." This wasn't, he fervently hoped, the beginning of a trend. "Good luck."

Paudie smiled. "Luck? Who needs luck?"

Me, thought Benny.

One by one they deserted him, picking their way through dancing couples, to the line of females on the other side. Adult chaperones prowled the dance floor, throwing hellfire-and-brimstone stares at anyone who seemed to be having too good a time. Benny knew the pressure was on him to make that journey. At this moment, walking on hot coals seemed a preferable option. It wasn't fair. He was doing his best to fit in with these farmers. He'd eaten the hairy burger, drunk the Lucozade, and he'd done the headbanging. Now they wanted him to indulge in a spot of self-mortification in front of a hundred Dubliners. He wouldn't do it. He wouldn't. . . . Not for a while anyway.

Benny followed the progress of the others from behind his fingers. It was pathetic what young lads had to go through just to dance with some girl. Paudie got himself sorted quick enough. Some punky one with a ring in her nose. But the poor Ahern twins were refused by every girl in the row, before shuffling off to the loo in disgrace.

No way, thought Benny. Not me. I'd rather sit here on my own than join the sad brigade in the toilet. They'd have to stay in there now until the set was over.

"Ahem!" Someone was doing some throat clearing in his direction. Benny glanced up, half-expecting Furty to be looming over him. But no. It was a girl. Oh my God! It was Babe. She was glaring at him defiantly.

"Well?" she said.

Benny swallowed. "Well, I . . . eh . . . How's it going there, pixie?"

"Is that it?" demanded Babe. "That's all you can say?"

Benny wanted to talk. He wanted to say something intelligent and witty, but his brain was still processing the images his eyes had beamed up. It was Babe, he knew by her voice. But it wasn't the Babe he knew. Or maybe it was, and he never knew it. Oh get it together, he told himself, you can argue with yourself later.

Babe obviously had had the best part of a boutique concealed in her rucksack, because she'd given herself an overhaul the likes of which you wouldn't see on one of them Yankee talk shows. For a start, the hat was gone. Babe's curly brown hair was pulled back from her face. And the face—it was, well, pretty. Benny didn't get into the shape of the eyes, or sprays of freckles or anything. He'd leave that sort of thing to Georgie. But she was definitely pretty. He had to give her that. She had packed away the baggy clothes and replaced them with a simple floral dress. She still had her Timberlands on, though, her one link to the old Babe.

"You look . . ." Benny stammered.

"Yes?"

"You look like a girl. Exactly like a girl."

Babe rolled her eyes, and for a second Benny thought he was going to get a dig in the ribs. Then she calmed down, automatically reaching up to adjust the bobble on her hat.

Benny pointed at her head. "You're not actually wearing—"

"I know that, townie."

"Okay, sorry." Benny had no idea why he was apologizing. He just felt it might be wise.

"I'm going over there," said Babe. "To sit with the other girls. I'll be over there, if anyone's looking for me. With the girls."

"Righto, pixie," said Benny. "I get the message. You'll be over there. I'm not a dullard."

"Sometimes I wonder," grumbled Babe, weaving across to the girls' side of the hall.

Benny watched her go. He felt like he was missing something here. Why couldn't people just talk straight to each other? At least with Furty you knew where you stood. But girls spent all their time making fun of you, and then asked you to be their business partner. And then just when you thought you were getting on all right, she had to go all schizophrenic. Benny saw a film once where this nun went around doing loads of holy stuff during the day, and then murdering chaps at night.

He shuddered. Just his luck to wind up with a psycho for a partner. A pretty psycho though. Now where did that thought come from? One minute he's thinking about psychos, and the next his brain is reminding him that Babe was pretty.

Benny glanced across the hall just to be sure he wasn't hallucinating this whole transformation. Babe was spearing him with a black stare. What was going on? If she wanted to talk to him, why was she over there? Suddenly Benny got it. It hit him over the head, like a wingback from Gorey once had. But that's another story. Babe wanted to dance. She wanted to dance with him. And she wanted him to ask. Benny could almost hear the ping as his cowlick sprang to attention. What could he do? There was no escape.

Benny rose to his feet in a daze. His whole body felt as though it were covered in a layer of sweat. He imagined a trail of soppy footprints leading back to his chair. It's okay, he told himself. No big deal. Just slide across inconspicuously, and have a quick dance. Nothing to it. As long as no one drew attention to him, he'd be fine.

"Go on, Shaw, ye boyo!" roared Paudie over his punkette partner's shoulder. Amplified by the hall's acoustics, the big farmer's voice sounded as though it were coming through a bullhorn.

"Thanks, buddy," said Benny weakly.

Every last person in that hall was now staring in his direction. He could feel the gaze of each seated girl flicker over him. Fresh meat. Ripe for humiliation. Come on, little boy. Ask me to dance. I dare you. Benny was almost relieved he already had a target.

But Babe was ignoring him. He was no more than ten feet away, heading directly for her, and she was staring off into space as though she had no clue what was going on. Benny took a deep breath. Time to get this over with. And suddenly some smarmy hip-hop type stepped in front of him. Benny felt an unexpected lurch in his stomach at the thought of someone else dancing with the pixie. He hung back. Babe would soon get rid of this chap.

"Howye there, good lookin'? Fancy an auld boogie?"

Babe smiled sweetly. Those who knew her would take this as a sign to run away. Quickly. "No, thanks."

The young chap would not be put off so easily. He had his reputation to consider. "Ah go on. I don't mind that ye'r only a culchie."

Benny winced. Surely the pixie would burst him now. But no. Babe was acting ladylike. "No, thanks. I'm grand, thanks."

Your man still wasn't getting the message. "Come on, now. A plain Jane like yerself can't get too many shots at a Romeo like me."

Babe casually dropped her drink can, and when the

gallant Romeo bent to retrieve it, she grabbed his earring.

"Listen, moron," she whispered. "If you don't go away, I'm going to beat you up in front of all your buddies, and you'll never dance in this town again."

The suitor blinked, uncertain if he'd actually heard what he thought he'd heard. One look into Babe's eyes confirmed it. He backed off hurriedly, colliding with a grinning Benny.

"I wouldn't bother, mate," he said. "That one's a right nettle."

Benny psyched himself up for the big question. He stepped in to the recently vacated space in front of his partner.

"Howye, pix . . . Babe?"

"Hello, Bernard." Bernard? Why did females go all formal when they were annoyed with him? "Can I help you with something?"

Benny had never been so nervous. Not when he was lining up the final shot of the county final. Not when he was flying around Tunisia with Omar on the back of a moped. Not even when he'd splashed petrol on his belly by accident and went around all day convinced that he was going to explode.

"I was wondering . . ."

"Hmm?"

"I was wondering, if you'd like to, you know . . ."

"No, Bernard. I'm afraid I don't know."

Bernard again? Had she been talking to his Ma?

"Dance!" he blurted. "Would you like to dance?"

Babe smiled. "Well, I don't generally dance with townies, but I suppose, seeing as you asked so nicely."

Benny was flummoxed. He'd thought he was doing Babe a favor. And now here he was feeling pathetically grateful. Babe grabbed his hand and yanked him onto the dance floor. Once there, they faced each other awkwardly.

"So, what's the story?" mumbled Benny.

Babe shrugged. "I don't know. Haven't you ever danced with a girl before?"

Benny sniffed. "'Course I have."

"Your ma, was it?"

"Yep. Look, this is my first disco. Have a bit of mercy, will you?"

"I've never danced with a boy, either," confessed Babe.

"A right pair we are," said Benny. "Well, what's everyone else doing?" They studied the other couples whirling around them. It seemed simple enough. Hands around the waist and a bit of an old sway. There were a few sets of old timers bursting around the perimeter, fancy footwork, twirls and everything. But that looked a bit complicated. Better stick to the basic method.

Muttering apologetically, Benny put his hands around

Babe's waist. He tried to accomplish this without actually touching her. She in turn put her hands on his shoulders. So far so good. They attempted a simple sway.

"This isn't too difficult, is it?"

Benny nodded, afraid to talk in case he lost his timing.

"Look happy, will you, for God's sake!"

Benny pulled his lips back in a mirthless grimace. How could you smile under this sort of pressure? They were spinning one way, everyone else was going the other, the hall seemed to be bouncing up and down. Music pulsed out of huge speakers, distorted by volume. His sweatshirt felt like a sponge, clinging wherever it touched his body. He was certain Babe's hands must be sopping where they made contact with him. Benny wasn't used to having anyone this close to him. She must be able to hear every sound his body made. Suddenly Benny's belly wouldn't stop rumbling. Strange bubbling and whistling spun around his intestines. Then he couldn't stop swallowing. His throat clicked and rasped with a ferocity he'd never noticed before. Babe must think he was some sort of freak.

They danced for what seemed like hours, but was probably only a few minutes. Benny had never been so glad to hear "The Birdy Song." They disentangled gingerly.

Babe had a strange smile on her face. "Well, now. That wasn't so bad."

Bad! thought Benny. Bad! It was terrible. A nightmare!

If I never set foot on a dance floor again, it'll be too soon. But out loud he said. "No. Not so bad."

They strolled back to their chairs to find the Ahern twins returned from the loo.

"All those girls are really ugly. I wouldn't dance with one of them," announced Seanie.

Sean nodded vehemently. "You're telling me. Heifers, the whole lot of them."

Babe giggled. "There's a much better selection in the boys' toilets, I suppose?"

The twins were mortified. There was an unspoken agreement among teenage boys that you never questioned a comrade's ability to get a dance. Now, all of a sudden, Babe turns into a girl and starts breaking the rules.

Now that Benny was sitting among the boys again, the dance didn't seem so bad. He felt the weary pride of someone who has survived boot camp. The Ahern twins weren't making any comments, either. He had attained a higher status, in the same bracket as Paudie. One of the mysterious group who had Danced With Girls.

There was one more slow set. By this time, Benny had worked himself up to another dance, but the Aherns decided that Babe owed them a spin around the floor, at the very least, for putting up with her all year. No sooner had the first warbly notes of "My Heart Will Go On" floated over the hall, than Sean and Seanie started scuffling for first go. Seanie won out, and, leaving his brother writing on the floor, he hauled Babe out for a dance. Babe was too surprised to refuse. Not that she was actually asked or anything.

The dance was more of a public relations exercise than an actual dance in its own right. Seanie wanted to show all the girls who regularly refused him that he was capable of getting a dance partner. This meant Babe had to be paraded past nearly every female in the hall. She was dragged around in a rugby-tackle clinch, while Seanie shouted abuse at the rest of the dancers: "You see now, do you? You missed out on this! You could have had me if you'd played your cards right."

Babe put up with this for two songs, before spiking Seanie's toe with her heel and hurrying back to the group. By this time Sean had recovered and was demanding his dance.

"My turn now."

"Turn? I'm not a video game. Get stuffed."

"Ah, go on. You danced with that other eejit."

"That other eejit is your identical twin."

"So?"

Babe sighed. "Well, if he's an eejit, then so . . . never mind. Oh, come on. Let's get it over with."

Seanie commiserated with Benny. "You see, this is what happens when you've got a pretty girlfriend."

"She's not my . . ." began Benny, then stopped. "Yes, I suppose. I suppose it is."

The boys were heading off to some yeehaw barbecue on the beach. Plenty of headbanging music guaranteed. Benny's ears were already ringing from the disco music. He was almost glad of an excuse to go home.

"Are you on, townie?"

"No, Paudie. I have to be back or this'll be my last disco for the summer."

"Babe?"

"Nope. If I'm not in by eleven, my parents will have air-sea rescue out looking for me."

Paudie swung a leg over his monster bike. "Right, so. See you during the week."

He pedaled off up the village street, the Aherns trailing behind like two faithful puppies.

The road to Duncade was dark. Once they outdistanced the orange glow of Newford's street lights, the only illumination besides their own lamps was the steady sweep of the lighthouse beam. A beacon to guide them home.

They rode quietly for a while, settling into a rhythm. It was strange how one little dance could change everything. Benny realized that Babe hadn't insulted him for ages, and it made him very uneasy.

There were no cars on the road. It would be quiet now

until closing time. Then the designated drivers would load up their vehicles with singing holidaymakers and ferry them to their hotel rooms or caravans.

"Well?" said Babe eventually.

"Well."

"Not a bad night, was it?"

Benny shook his head, trying to dislodge the heavy metal that was still banging around in there. "No, not a bad night."

"Those two eejits nearly broke every one of my toes with their big gawky feet."

Benny laughed. "That was funny, all right. Those boys were desperate."

"Is that so?"

Benny groaned. "No, Babe, that's not what I meant. This is terrible. I don't know what to say to you now you're a girl."

"Go 'way!" said Babe, her voice dripping with sarcasm. "I thought you were doing really well."

"Everything I say turns out as an insult. You never minded that before, but now . . ."

"Now?"

"Well, now it's like insulting . . . you know, a real girl."

"Benny."

"What?"

"Shut up!"

"Fair enough."

A bike ride goes by quickly enough when your head is full of music and memories. Benny had no clue what little plans were circulating in the pixie's devious female head, but he was certain that he played a part in there somewhere. At least, he hoped so. Imagine the faces on the boys at home when he informed them that he'd been hanging around with a girl all summer. Would they be jealous or disgusted? He wasn't sure. Benny grinned in the darkness. He didn't care.

In no time, it seemed, they crested the far side of Church Hill, and free-wheeled down to the pump. Benny dismounted and cranked the ancient handle. The first splash of water was coppery, then it flowed crystal clear.

"After you," he said gallantly.

Babe studied him bemusedly. "It's still me, townie. Me in a dress. You don't have to be doing all this Lancelot stuff."

"Fair enough," said Benny, shoving his head under the stream.

"Ah well," sighed Babe. "It was nice while it lasted."

A lone light crawled over the hill. The sputtering of a motorbike engine rumbled down to their ears.

"A bike," commented Babe. "Now what's he doing stopped up there?"

Benny shook water from his hair. "What?"

"There's some lad on a motorbike up there. Just sitting."

Benny squinted into the gloom. It was no use, all he could see was a headlight. "You know who has a bike?"

Babe groaned. "Don't say it."

"I'm afraid so. Furty Howlin."

As if on cue, an eerie cry pierced the darkness.

"Benneeeeeeeee!"

"Oh no! He's gone mental!"

"Baaaaaabe!"

Benny jumped on his racer. "Let's go!"

Babe stuck out her lip. "No. I'm not running."

"Use your brain, pixie. Dark night. Reform school. No Conger. No witnesses."

Babe pondered it for a moment. "Okay. Stand and fight another day."

They slipped down into first gear and pedaled up the far side of Church Hill. It was painfully obvious that they were never going to outdistance a motorbike, but they had no choice except to try. Behind them, the bike's engine changed pitch as Furty dropped her out of neutral. He was giving chase!

Benny stood up out of the saddle, pumping the pedals as fast as possible. The rumble of the engine grew nearer at a frightening pace, the bike's headlight throwing Benny's and Babe's shadows on the road ahead. In seconds, Furty had caught them and was revving at their heels. Teasing them.

"I thought we'd play a game of cat and mouse," he shouted over the engine's roar. "You two can be the mice. And here's the cat."

Benny risked a sideways glance. In his gloved hand, Furty held aloft a dead cat. Its midriff was flattened and lined with tire tread. Benny cursed car drivers who couldn't spot a fleeing cat.

"Oh no!" he muttered.

Somehow, Babe heard. "What? What is it?"

"Don't look," Benny grunted. "Keep pedaling."

Babe looked, 'course she did. Wouldn't you? Word-less-ly, she put her head down, and increased her pace.

Furty laughed. He drew alongside the cyclists, swinging the cat over his head. It was terrifying to catch sight of him out of the corner of your eye, hoping that he wouldn't throw his disgusting missile, knowing that he would. The lighthouse lamp etched his features in stark black and white. Furty was elated, wind and joy stretching his lips back in a feral grin.

Benny took the first blow. The wet corpse slapped into his shoulder, driving him into the ditch. Thorns and twigs scratched his face and clothing. But Benny didn't care, he just wanted away from that cat. His bike clattered to the tarmac, spokes spinning in the lamp light. Benny jumped to his feet, face distorted in disgust. He slapped his clothing, as though parts of the cat remained there.

"Give it up, Furty!" he shouted, an outraged tremor in his voice. "That's enough! Do you hear me?"

Furty circled around to reclaim the cat's body. "Enough? Are you joking me? I'm only getting started."

He gunned the bike and set off after Babe. Benny righted his racer, and pursued them.

Furty couldn't. He wouldn't. Not to a girl. But Furty would and did. Babe was trapped like a rabbit in the bully's headlight. Benny arrived just in time to see her topple to the road, the cat wrapped grotesquely around her neck. He dismounted on the move, running to his partner's aid.

"You okay?"

"Get it off me!"

Benny plucked gingerly at the sticky corpse, and lobbed it over the ditch. "Now! That's the end of your stupid game."

Furty flicked down his kickstand. "Not at all, townie. That just buys you a few seconds' head start." He clambered over the ditch to reclaim his weapon.

Benny pulled at Babe's shoulders. "Come on! Hurry up!"

Babe was still shaking. "What?"

"We have to get away!"

Babe staggered to her feet. "That . . ." She couldn't find words to describe her disgust.

"Never mind that now! We've got to put some distance between ourselves and Furty."

But Babe wasn't leaving without some token retribution. She looked around wildly for a stick, a rock, anything. Her gaze landed on Furty's idling bike.

"Right!" she said, rubbing her palms.

"Pixie! No! You'll just make him worse!"

"Worse! How could he be worse?"

Benny paused. How could you argue with that?

Babe put her shoulder into the bike's petrol tank and heaved it onto its side. The crash was amplified by the still night air. And the last thing picked out by the headlight before it fizzled out, was Furty's horrified face bobbing up behind the hedge.

"Put that in your pipe and smoke it," shouted the not-so-ladylike-anymore Babe Meara. She turned to Benny, the flush on her cheeks evident even in the darkness. "Right. Let's go before he gets over that hedge."

Benny didn't need to be asked twice. They pedaled furiously down the winding road, only the pale disks of light from their lamps saving them from crashing, head-first, into several thorny ditches. Benny felt a stitch cutting into his side. It started as a pinprick, then spread like a live wire across his abdomen. He had to keep going. Get through to his second wind.

The sound of Furty's curses cut through the wind in his

ears. Benny smiled grimly. There might be a high price to pay for that little gesture. The motorbike took up the pursuit again. Benny swore he could feel it vibrating through the tarmac. At least this time Furty was riding blind.

"Benny," hissed Babe. "Lights out. Quick!"

Benny complied, and the world was plunged into darkness, even the light from the moon seeming too feeble to reach the earth.

"Into the ditch!"

Benny hesitated for a second. He'd been in the ditch already, and it wasn't a pleasant experience. He weighed it against having a dead cat stuffed down his gullet. On reflection, the ditch didn't seem too bad.

They stepped down into the mystery greenery off the road, pulling their bikes in behind them. At the bottom of the channel, a soggy marsh squelched through their shoes and crawled up past their shins. Wet leaves slapped their faces, and a hundred insects and airborne critters latched on to any patch of exposed skin.

"Nice idea, pixie."

"Shut up. Here he comes."

Benny held his breath, using his body to shield the shiny frame of his racer. Shine up your bike, Da had said, so you'll be visible at night. Thanks very much, Da.

Furty roared past them, a dark bulky shadow. Benny could make out the limply dangling shape of the cat in his left fist. In the sweep of the lighthouse they once more saw his features. A mask of frustration and hate.

"What happened to that guy?" Benny wondered again. "We used to be friends."

"Shhhh! He's coming back!"

The roar of the engine grew louder. Furty had obviously figured out their little ruse.

"Benneeeee! Baaaaaabe! I know you're close! I'll find you!"

Benny resisted the urge to take a swipe at a spider that was heading for his nostril.

"Come out and face me! Are you chicken or something?"

Benny felt Babe stiffen beside him. She was just about crazy enough to go out there. He put a hand on her shoulder.

"No," he whispered, the merest breath of air. "No, Babe."

She relaxed, settling back into the brackish water.

Furty slowed to a crawl, his tires crunching gravel. "I know where you are. I know exactly. And I'll give you a ten-second head start, then I'm coming in!"

It was a bluff. Hopefully.

And then Furty was there. Right in front of them. His frame frozen in the tower light. His nose was lifted, as though he could sniff them out. Benny and Babe hugged each other for courage. Furty's gaze swung like a periscope, scrutinizing every inch of scrub. He must see them. He must! They were crouched not three feet from the bike's front wheel.

"All right, then. Here we go. One, two . . ."

He began the countdown. Slowly and ominously. Benny started to shake. Maybe Furty did know where they were. Maybe he could see them as plain as day. No, he told himself. People like Furty don't give head starts. If he knew where they were, they'd be tasting dead cat right this minute.

". . . eight, nine, ten! Here I come!"

But he didn't come, because the whole thing had been a bluff after all.

"To hell with you two!" he swore. "I've better things to do than sit around here all night. But don't worry, there's always tomorrow."

And with that, he opened up the throttle, prodded the bike into first gear, and roared off toward Duncade.

They didn't speak for several seconds. It could be a trick.

"I hate him, I'm not telling a lie," said Benny at last.

"Me too," said Babe, climbing out of the ditch. She shook her soaked Timberlands in disgust. "Sort of takes the good out of the night doesn't it?"

"Yep."

They cycled silently, still shaken by the night's events.

"We're going to have to sort something out."

"I know. What, though?"

Benny chewed his lip. "I don't know. I'll have to ask Granda."

"What about your Da?"

"Da? No. He'd just go up to Furty's house and beat the door down. We have to handle this ourselves."

"Agreed."

What were they doing? wondered Benny. Deciding that they should handle Furty themselves. His father couldn't handle him. The police couldn't, and even reform school didn't appear to have done such a great job. But the brave Benny and Babe were going to have a lash at it. Madness. Utter madness. But at the same time it made perfect sense. Once parents got involved, things would rapidly explode out of all proportion. There'd be no more discos for a start. And no more going over the rocks. No doubt a feud would erupt between the Shaws and the Howlins. In six generations they wouldn't even remember why they were killing each other. It was all right to ask Granda, though. He wasn't an adult. Not really. He was past all that.

"Oh no!" snarled Babe, getting less ladylike by the second.

"What is it?" asked Benny alarmed.

"The Kimberleys," she replied. "We've left them behind the pump."

7

MASK AND FLIPPERS

Granda was fixing a bearing on the tower lens when they went to see him.

"Captain? Have you got a minute?"

"Nope," said Paddy Shaw around the screwdriver between his teeth. "Work to do."

He pointed at the console. "Push that blue button."

Benny's finger hovered over the complicated array of controls. He chose one.

"No, for God's sake, no! That's the self destruct!"

Benny jerked his hand away.

Babe shook her head in disgust. "Sucker."

"Oh, come on up, the two of you," chuckled Granda.

They scaled the metal steps and into the actual lamp. It was like sitting inside a giant bulb. The outside world warped and blurred through the tooled lenses. The meager jot of Irish sun seemed almost Mediterranean.

"Wow," said Babe.

"Wow is right, Scut," said Granda, screwing a panel over a lattice of wires. "So, how was the hop last night? Tell me, now, are you two mods or rockers?" He winked to show he was in touch with the younger generation.

"Granda. We have a bit of a problem."

"Furty Howlin, is it?"

Benny blinked. "How did you know?"

"Jerry Bent told me," said Granda, straight-faced.

Babe snorted. "But he's only able to say 'butterflies'."

"Sucker," sniggered Benny.

"It's a small village. Someone sees everything. I noticed the little confrontation at the arch the other morning. What's his problem?"

"He says we're poaching his lures."

"He's the poacher," Babe interjected. "Putting down lure traps all over the place."

"Lure traps," frowned Paddy Shaw. "That's bad news. Gets the whole village a bad name."

"He's trying to put us out of business."

"Well, the way he sees it, you're putting him out of business."

"What?"

Granda sat on the rubber mat beside them. "Let me tell you something about Furty Howlin. Since getting out of Julian's, he's asked every captain in a twenty-mile radius for a job. Nobody will touch him. With the amount of overfishing that's going on, it's hard enough making ends meet without having someone you don't trust on the deck."

"It's his own fault," interrupted Babe.

Granda nodded. "Maybe so. But for a sixteen-year-old country lad, not to be earning is a great embarrassment. Most of the other fellows his age are bringing home the bones of two hundred quid a week. So for him, lure hunting is the bottom of the barrel. And now, he doesn't even have that to himself."

"So, what are we supposed to do? Give up lure hunting because Furty's depressed?"

Granda grinned. "God, Scut, you're hard-faced, all right. Did you ever consider a career in psychiatry?"

"No. I'm putting all my energy into the high jump."

"I'm beginning to see why Furty wants to throttle the pair of you."

Benny was getting a bit frustrated with all these jibes. Couldn't anybody he knew just have a straight conversation?

"Granda? Are you going to help us or not?"

Paddy Shaw scratched his stubble thoughtfully. "You see, Benny. There is, inside us all, a power. A force. Use the force, Luke . . . I mean Benny, use the force."

Babe buried her face in her hands. "I thought fishermen were too ruggedly tough to be robbing lines from Yankee movies."

"What lines?" protested Granda.

"Come on, Granda. This is serious. He chased us with a dead cat last night."

Granda shrugged. "Sure, how fast can a dead cat run?"

Benny counted to ten. "He didn't chase us with a dead cat. He threw the cat at us."

"Oh."

"So, Captain," said Babe. "Any chance of a bit of advice there, or would we be better off chatting to Jerry Bent?"

"I can see why you're hanging around with this young lady, Benny. She's a real charmer."

"You should see her playing hurling."

"Are you two finished?"

Granda wiped the oil from his fingers with a rag. "You need to find something you can do and Furty can't. That way you're not in competition with him."

"Like what?"

"I don't know. Something to do with lures. Don't back down altogether. Adapt. That's the key to survival. The Irish fisherman is the perfect example."

They knew there was a story coming, but Granda made them wait, rolling a pencil-thin cigarette.

"Back in the fifties, the fish were jumping out of the water in Duncade. The mackerel would come into the dock maybe twenty times a year. All you'd have to do was drop down a bucket on a rope into the water and you'd come up with a few dozen mackerel. Fish, being the stupidest creatures in creation, didn't even know enough to swim out on the tide. So when the dock emptied, they died in their thousands. It was like a silver blanket on the strand. You could see the glare from the Saltee Islands."

Granda took a drag on his cigarette, eyes lost in the memory.

"Sure, then you got overfishing European trawlers coming into our waters, and factory effluents, not to mention falling prices. A lesser breed would have been wiped out. Not the Irish, though. No way. What did they do?"

"They adapted," intoned Benny and Babe automatically.

"Yep. Certainly did. Went after the crustaceans. Mussels, lobsters, shrimp, crabs, and crayfish. Those shellfish thrive on a bit of pollution. Mutate into big jumbos. Do you see my point?"

Blank stares all around.

Granda sighed. "The point is that they didn't give up the fishing altogether. They just shifted the goalposts a bit."

Babe arched an eyebrow. "And this would help us— how exactly?"

"What is it you can do that Furty can't?"

"I dunno. There must be something."

"Well, think about it. I'm sure a pair of obnoxious smart alecks like yourselves will come up with something."

Granda climbed down the steps on to the deck. "Here's something that usually helps me to think."

He flicked back a protective cover and pressed a red button. Slowly the pulleys operating the lens swung into life. Benny and Babe sat transfixed as the giant panes of bevelled glass revolved around them. The world was transformed. Clouds bled into mountains like streaks of luminous paint. Sunlight etched the edges of the glass and exploded into rainbow brilliance. Benny had seen it a hundred times before, but how could anyone tire of a panorama such as this? It was Babe's first time.

"Swim," said Benny, when the dome eventually halted.

"Huh?" slurred Babe, still a bit dopey from the experience.

"Well, as far as I can remember, Furty Howlin always hated getting in the water. He's not able to swim."

Babe's eyes focused, and a sly grin crept across her face. "Hmmm," she said thoughtfully.

A fisherman not being able to swim. A totally implausible plot point, you may think. But no! A surprisingly high percentage of mariners actually believe it's bad luck to learn how to stay afloat on the high seas. Not only can they not swim, but they won't even permit life jackets on their vessels. If you can swim, then you're just tempting fate to whip up a storm and make you swim. Not exactly Spocklike logic. But in spite of statistics, and the triumph of science over superstition in most areas, many fishermen have never immersed their bodies in anything larger than a bath.

Benny and partner were sitting on Horatio's Bridge, legs dangling over the precipice. They had, on Babe's insistence, brought their snorkeling gear along. Currents whipped the tide into a froth. Yellow spume floated skywards on the wind.

"It was never yellow before," commented Babe. "That's from all those factories up the coast, pumping all sorts of chemicals into the sea."

"That's illegal, isn't it?"

Babe gave him a townies-are-so-dumb look. "Yeah, sure. It's illegal. I suppose that means nobody's doing it?"

Conger yipped in agreement, trying again to nudge Benny over the edge.

"Hey, mutt! I thought we were friends now!"

"That is friendly. Remember what he did to the eel?"

Benny nodded. "True. Now, explain this plan to me again."

Babe rubbed her temples. Why could these townies never grasp something the first time around? "Your Granda said to find something that Furty couldn't do. Right?"

"Right."

"So you said he can't swim."

"Okay. With you so far."

"And we can swim."

"True."

"So, we should use this ability to our advantage."

"Yes?"

Babe pointed to the turquoise cauldron beneath them. "So, here we are."

Benny frowned. "I think you've skipped a step there, pixie."

They were back to insulting each other again. It didn't have the same sting in it, though. Not since the disco. A bond had been formed by the trauma of having a deceased cat hurled at them. That and the dance. Benny noticed that Babe had left her woolly hat at home. The sea breeze streamed her chestnut hair out behind her. Looked like she was a girl permanently. Good or bad? Good. Definitely good.

Babe sighed. "Look down there, townie. What do you see?"

Benny stared between his Reeboks. Twenty feet below, the channel widened to an oval pool. Horseshoe shelves descended into the glittering depths. Flashes of azure and emerald phosphorescence pierced the surface. "Eh . . . water."

"Duh."

"Well, what am I supposed to say?"

"Look under your behind, townie."

Benny checked under his jeans. On the rock, in white emulsion, was the number seven and a large star. "So?"

"Those numbers are markers. The seven tells all the Dubs that this here is a good fishing rock. The star means it's a safe area. No blow holes or freak waves. This place is thronged every night."

"That's not a whole lot of use to us, seeing as the pool never empties out, even at ebb tide."

Babe tapped her forehead. "Ah yes, but we can swim, can't we?"

"You want to go snorkeling in there?"

"I'm telling you, it's a goldmine. That hole has never been done. There's a fortune down there."

"I don't know, Babe."

"You could get your boots next weekend."

Unfair tactics. Babe knew how weak he was when it came to cash.

"Okay. We'll have a go."

They separated to change. Benny began to get a bit self-conscious pulling on his denim shorts. His knees were covered in scabs as usual. And he had that half-baked tan that didn't extend past his wrists or ankles. Not exactly your beach-god type. Them boys all had big ripply muscles hopping off their chests. The only thing sticking out of Benny's torso were his bony ribs. There was only one thing to do. He would have to plunge into Horatio's Pool before Babe got a glimpse of his milk-white frame.

"Well, townie? Are you ready or what?"

Babe was standing behind him, a translucent yellow mask pulled down over her face. Her curly hair was stuffed into a blue swimming hat, giving her a Marge Simpson look.

Benny yelped. "You shouldn't sneak up on people when they're getting changed!"

"Oh, stop your whining and come on."

Picking his way down the rocky incline, Benny reckoned that Babe looked so dopey in that getup he didn't have anything to worry about.

They sat on the pool's edge pulling on their flippers. Babe removed her mask and spat on the lens.

"Saliva keeps down the condensation," she explained.

"Charming."

"Well, if a shark sneaks up on you, don't blame me."

Benny gurgled a large ball of spittle in the back of his throat and deposited it into his mask.

Babe grimaced in disgust. "Just a drop, townie. There's no need to fill the thing up."

Benny was particularly proud of his mask. It had three faces for wraparound view. A birthday present from his Granda.

He dipped a flippered toe into the surf. It was freezing. "That's freezing!" he exclaimed.

"Quiet!" ordered Babe dramatically. "I think I heard a chicken clucking."

Benny chuckled. The pixie never let up. His toe was becoming accustomed to the water, so he tried an entire foot. He suppressed a gasp. It was going to take a few minutes to lower himself into the pool.

Babe stood, turned, and with her fingers spread across the face of her mask, jumped backward into the water. A Babe-shaped hole appeared in the foam. And of course the foam that used to be in the hole splattered all over Benny. A dollop even landed in his snorkel, trickling down to his mouth. He spat it out, scraping his tongue against his teeth.

Conger went in off a high ledge. He pinwheeled excitedly in midair and splashed down beside his master. The splash, naturally, went all over Benny. At least it washed off the foam.

Benny took a deep rubbery breath through the snorkel. The dog had shamed him. No one would care that Conger had a fur coat, and so didn't feel the chill of the water. They'd just laugh because a dog got in before him.

He eased himself off the shelf. The water inched up his body like an icy knife. His breath came in short breaths, and he was convinced that crystalized clouds must be puffing from the snorkel's tube.

Babe had crossed the pool and was sitting on a shelf under the bridge. The gentle swell raised and lowered her like a giant heartbeat. Benny kicked over to her, glad to be free of the foam's sticky fingers.

"Down here," chattered Babe through blue lips. "The boys throw out lines from the point, right under the bridge. It's a good cast if you can make it. Dangerous though. Too far and you foul in the rocks. If you don't reel in fast enough, the lure pulls you down into the weeds."

Benny spat out his mouthpiece. "Hopefully."

They adjusted the seals on their masks and peered under the surface. The orange moss reflected the sunlight, and you'd swear the water was lovely and warm, if you weren't sitting in it. Not much life. A few crawlies scuttled across sandy patches, and the odd sprat flitting along the rock face.

Benny kicked away from the plate and floated on his stomach, paddling hands to stay in position.

"I see one!" he said, or he meant to say. Because he had a snorkel in his gob, what he actually said was, "Aye-ee-uu."

Taking a deep breath, he threw his legs up and stiffened his body like a steel rod. His aqua-dynamic shape took him straight down. Cold enveloped him instantly. That and pressure. He felt a mild pain in his ears, and an invisible band being tightened across his chest. He had about thirty seconds before that band succeeded in squeezing the air from his lungs.

It was a different world beneath the sun-warmed surface. One that you couldn't understand from watching the television. Maybe you could see the change in light, but you could never appreciate the instantaneous prickling of your skin with a million goose bumps, or the casual dragging of your body by irresistible currents.

Benny kicked, the flippers multiplying the power of his legs. He allowed the air to trickle between his lips, rising to the surface in a ropelike stream. The water resisted his presence, trying to propel him upward, but Benny lengthened his kick and streaked to the seabed.

The flash he had spotted was a Caster gold, its triple hook snagged on a razor-sharp rock shelf. Whoever lost it had put up a tremendous fight, pulling one of the barbs almost straight. Benny unhooked it gingerly, then allowed the air in his lungs to carry him upward. Babe floated above him, her pale limbs waving lazily, and Conger was pedalling in erratic circles. Benny could see the land and sky folding overhead, as though viewed through some funhouse mirror. For a moment he believed that he could stay in this underwater kingdom forever. He would never need oxygen, and he would never be cold. Then his brain reminded him that it was probably oxygen deprivation that had him thinking these dopey thoughts in the first place.

He broke the surface, sucking down a giant gulp of air. "Look," he gasped. "A Caster gold."

But Babe was gone—he turned just in time to see the tips of her fins slide beneath the surface. Benny swam to the shallows, laying the lure carefully above the tideline. Babe was right, as usual; this was a gold mine. And Furty couldn't be jealous. They weren't cutting across him. This was a place he could never go, and probably wouldn't want to.

Furty was chuckling away to himself at the dead-cat episode. It was the first thing to bring a sincere smile to his face since he got out. That shut the pair of them up. Even Babe Meara didn't have a smart-aleck comment ready for that particular situation. Pity about the cat, though. Furty liked cats. Admired them for their independence and cunning. Your average cat survived on its wits. A cat didn't need any stupid trawler captain to give it a job, and it certainly didn't wait around for any useless waster of a parent to provide for it. If Furty could be any animal, he decided, he'd like to be a cat. He shook himself. What sort of rubbish was that? He'd like to be a cat? That was the stupid sort of fairy-story thinking that Shaw's mother went on with. He wasn't a cat. Never would be. So there was no point in inventing stupid stories in his head.

Furty's mood was buoyed by the fact that he'd had

quite a decent haul over the rocks. He was sure that the other two would have picked them clean like a gull on a fish head. Especially as he'd slept through the early tide. It had been late afternoon before he'd passed through the arch, dismally certain that the only thing he'd return with would be a few rusty feathers, and whatever his trap yielded. Contrary to what he'd boasted, Furty was still scouring the rocks as well as hauling his trap. He couldn't believe his luck when he'd plucked a jumbo German out of the weed at the Babby's Pool. Just lying there. Barely concealed by a strand of rack. Those two must be blind as bats if they missed that one.

A thought struck him. Maybe his terror tactics had actually worked. Could it be possible that he'd actually scared that pair off? Furty blinked. It couldn't be true. In his experience, all his little schemes had ever brought him was retaliation. But maybe this time. After all, he wasn't dealing with anyone hard here. Just two blow-in bigmouths. Maybe the cat thing had pushed them over the edge. Furty realized that he didn't feel any better. He was still angry. He just wasn't sure who with.

Furty didn't go directly into the house, he circled around the back to the shed.

This used to be quite an impressive workshop. All the local boys would come around with broken stuff for his Da to mend. An outboard engine, a brass compass, or on one occasion, a hunting rifle. Didn't matter what. Da would look at it, say: "No way, there's no way I can fix that one," and then disappear into the shed for half the night. Ma would criticize him but be half delighted at the same time.

Furty picked up an old biscuit tin. The drill bits inside were rusted and useless. The place was a dump now. Da hadn't done a job for years. It was at the stage now where Da's old buddies weren't even trying to persuade him to go back to work.

Furty pulled back an old tarpaulin and fumbled around for his lure box. Even before he opened it, he knew something was wrong. It should be heavy, dragging along the floor. There should be over two hundred lures in there. Furty hadn't sold one of his lures. Not one. He was saving them for the bank holiday weekend. For weeks he'd been searching not only the Duncade rocks, but biking over to Slade and Duncannon as well.

The plan was to make a big killing, clearing enough for a deposit on a bedsit in Dublin. He'd met a guy in Saint Julian's. A Dub who knew someone with cheap rooms. A fresh start. Away from drunks and fishermen and small-town know-it-alls. In Dublin he'd be plain old Furty Howlin. Furty Howlin with a future and no past.

But the box was light. Light enough to be empty. Furty felt a pallor sweep across his face. It couldn't be. He pulled the box out. It was empty! Empty! Furty closed his eyes for a long moment and looked again. Still empty. His nightmare had come true.

He knew what had happened. His brain told him, and his twisted gut told him. The same thing that had happened to all Ma's old jewelery. The same thing that had happened to Furty's own record collection when he'd been away. The same thing that had happened to everything valuable in the house.

Furty hurled the box on the cracked concrete floor. But it wasn't enough. A rage had a hold on him now. He picked up a rusted crowbar and swept the tools from the shelves. He smashed the window and battered the workbench until his arms were sore. Tears dripping from his nose, Furty stormed into the house.

His Da was slumped in a threadbare armchair in front of a cold grate.

"Where's me lures?" demanded Furty.

Jonjo Howlin raised a droopy eyelid. "Howye, son? Good day, had ye?"

"Never mind that! Me lures? What have you done with them?"

"Lures? What lures would that be?"

"The lures in the shed! You know what I'm talking about!"

Jonjo Howlin ran his tongue along his teeth, wincing at

the taste. "Don't make me get up out of this seat now, boy. You're not too old for a lick of the leather."

Furty snorted. "I am too old. Too old for you, anyway. And I don't think anything short of a miracle could get you up out of that seat."

His Da shook his head. "No respect. That was always your problem. No respect for nothing." Jonjo Howlin pulled a bottle of whiskey from behind the cushion and poured himself a shaky shot.

"That's good stuff," exclaimed Furty. "Where'd you get the money for that?"

"Hmm?"

"The whiskey. How could you afford that?"

His father studied him curiously. For his addled brain, this was the beginning of a new conversation. Furty was often convinced that Jonjo Howlin didn't even recognize his own son. "The whiskey?"

"Yes. Where did you get the money?"

Jonjo concentrated. "The money? Oh, I sold a box of old lures out in the shed. Some stupid tourist gave me a tenner for them. Eejit."

Furty shuddered. His future was gone. Sold for a bottle of whiskey. A fraction of its value. It would take him months to build up his stock again. Especially with competition. Furty felt the fight drain out of him. His shoulders rounded and his chin drooped. His own father.

Jonjo Howlin took another swig of alcohol. "Here, son. Make us some beans on toast, will you? I'm a bit peckish after today."

Furty nodded, defeated. "Okay, Da. Beans on toast it is, then."

"Good lad. You're not so bad as some would have me believe."

Furty shuffled into the kitchen. He knew he'd have to shake his father awake for the meal, and possibly carry him to bed after it. Then he'd have the night to mourn the loss of his bait collection. He'd just have to start from scratch. There was no way around it. He paused, his hand hovering over the fridge door. No way, except one.

8

SQUARE PEGS

The sub-aqua diving idea was a fantastic success. Babe claimed responsibility, seeing as it was actually her idea. Benny claimed credit because it was his Granda that had encouraged them to think of an idea. And he had thought of swimming. Benny, of course, was a past master at claiming credit for things he was only marginally connected to. He'd once claimed responsibility for a goal because he'd taken the dive that won the free kick!

On that first morning, they managed to salvage thirty-six saleable lures from the diving pool. Nearly fifty more were too ravaged by the brine to be of any value. Some had obviously been underwater for years. It was a tremendous coup for the Shaw-Meara Conglomerate. They had actually upped their recovery average without stepping on anyone's toes. Furty had the rocks, they had the pool. Everyone was happy. Well, that was the theory anyway.

And all the time Benny's little stash was growing. He

squandered a few bob on choc-ices and discos, but generally, Benny Shaw was proving to be quite the little Scrooge. When Georgie asked him how many spirits had visited him last Christmas, Benny would have issued a few punches if he'd got the joke.

Jessica Shaw was getting a bit worried about her little man. The euphoria she'd felt over Benny meeting a girl had passed once she actually got to know Babe. Not only was the local lass not as . . . well, feminine as she would have liked, but Bernard seemed to be transforming Babe into a miniature model of himself. When they weren't up the rocks dragging lures out of the weed, they were knocking sparks off each other playing that hurling game. Not exactly Romeo and Juliet. More like Bonnie and Clyde.

So, she resolved, it was up to her to inject some culture into their primeval existences. They would, Jessica was certain, love it once they got a taste. Well, she wasn't absolutely certain, but Benny would thank her in his Oscar speech.

The partners in question were whacking a sliotar around in the sheep field, much to the annoyance of the residents, who were sick of getting pelted with the hurling ball.

Babe was having trouble with her pick-up.

"You're not supposed to be digging a trench, you know," Benny shouted, as Babe once again buried the tip of her hurley in the muck.

"Watch it, townie!"

Benny casually rolled the ball on to his hurley. "You see, that's your whole problem right there!"

"What's my problem right there?"

"The culchie-townie thing. You crowd, farmers that is, are what I call hackers. You bull in, drooling away, and pull on the ball, or someone's legs, or whatever happens to be in the way. There's no grace, no subtlety."

Babe tutted. "Read a book, have you?"

"I have not!" said Benny defensively.

"Are you going to show me this pick-up you're always going on about, or are you going to give me another lecture?"

Benny did not appreciate accusations of being learned, so he decided to demonstrate.

"Watch."

Benny placed the sliotar on a tuft of grass and took several paces backward. He trotted toward the ball, his hurley almost scraping the ground. But instead of scooping the sliotar from underneath, he whacked the ball on the noggin and caught it on the hop. It was undeniably an impressive maneuver, spoiled only by a half-hidden root that tripped young Benny as he swanned past. That and the cowpat that permeated his jersey on impact.

Babe made no attempt whatsoever to smother a giggle. "Is that part of the move?"

Benny lay still, wondering if he should fake injury to avoid Babe's teasing. His mother's voice made up his mind for him. "Bernard! What on earth . . . ?"

Bernard? What was Ma doing here? It wasn't allowed. This was his place. You didn't catch him invading her women's meetings. Now the only two females that he actually held conversations with were waiting to see the splatter pattern on his good jersey. Reluctantly, he peeled himself off the ground, holding the destroyed garment away from his body.

Jessica and Babe were standing before him, both adopting an identical hands-on-hips stance. Spooky stuff.

"Showing off again, Bernard, are we?" said Jessica.

"When will you ever learn, Bernard?" added Babe, with a look of total disgust on her face.

"Hold on there now a second!"

"Yes, Bernard?"

Benny opened his mouth to say something smart. Something that would shut the pair of them up and leave him looking masterful. His gob hung open waiting for the brain to send a caustic comment, but it never arrived. How could you overcome half a kilogram of cow dung dripping off your shirt?

"Nothing, Ma . . ."

"Ma, Bernard? Ma?"

"Sorry . . . Mam."

Jessica shook her head. "Well, this has made up my mind for me. Look at you, covered in . . . that. You're a caveman, Bernard. My own little troglodyte!"

"I couldn't agree more," said Babe.

Jessica smiled at her. "I'm glad to see you've taken that filthy cap off, Babe. You have such lovely hair. Women in France pay a fortune for curls like that." Her scrutinizing stare traveled down over Babe's clothes. Baggy old sweatshirt and jeans. Both encrusted with fish scales. "There's still a bit of work to be done, though."

Benny frowned. This was going somewhere. Somewhere he didn't want it to go.

"So. I've made a little decision," announced Jessica.

Benny wondered would he agree with the word "little."

"I've decided that we're going to put on a play."

Benny reeled. "What?"

"A play, Bernard. A show. You, Babe, George, and myself."

"But, Mam! What did I do?"

Jessica smiled indulgently. "It's not a punishment, Bernard. It's to help broaden your horizons."

"My horizons are grand, thanks very much. They're as broad as a . . . broad thing." Benny's simile skills were letting him down again.

"Oh, stop being so selfish, Bernard. Think about someone else for a change. Maybe Babe is fed up bashing a smelly ball around the place."

"Babe?" scoffed Benny. "Sure, she's worse than me! Babe loves smelly things, and dogs and knives and all boys' stuff. Sure, Babe isn't like a girl at all." Once again Benny's tongue was operating independently of his brain. If he'd been watching Babe's face, he might have realized that he was on the wrong track.

"Oh really, Bernard? Why don't we let Babe decide?"

Babe was already fed up with Benny for his comments, and now here was this glamorous lady asking her to put on a play, of all things. Now, generally Babe would walk several miles in her bare feet to avoid drama or poetry or reading of any sort. But lately she'd been thinking more and more about the actual process of being a girl. And though she'd endure torture before admitting it, she'd actually had a go with her mother's lipstick. Added to this was the fact that Benny's mother looked sort of like someone that Babe might sort of want to be like . . . maybe, sort of.

So she said. "Yes. A play. I never did a play. Okay."

Jessica positively beamed. "Good girl. Now, Bernard! Maybe you don't know your friends as well as you think."

Benny was speechless. Maybe he didn't.

"Now, chin up, Babe. And straighten those shoulders. Stand like that and you'll have spine curvature before you're forty."

Benny's voice came rushing back. "Don't listen to her, Babe. She's trying to turn you into a . . ."

"Into a what, Bernard?"

Benny struggled to think of the worst possible insult. Something that would put Babe off this drama nonsense forever. "She's trying to turn you into a . . . big frilly blouse!"

Judging by the big sour looks on the two women's faces, he'd said the wrong thing yet again. Benny sighed. Looked like they were putting on a show.

Jessica draped an arm around Babe's shoulder and led her toward the lighthouse. They began whispering and giggling. Benny heard the word "neanderthal" mentioned, and wondered who they could be talking about. He moped along behind, cranking up his martyr act to the limit. Two females and himself, the odd man out.

Though Jessica had nothing but good intentions, the decision to immerse her eldest in culture was to set off a chain of events that would end in considerable heartache. That's not fair, really—blaming Jessica. Furty was the one who took advantage of the situation.

"I have come to rescue the princess from the Vampire King," muttered Benny.

Jessica rubbed a spot between her eyes. "What was that, honey?"

Benny raised his voice a notch. "The princess. I'm wanting to rescue her."

Jessica consulted her script. "That's not what it says here."

"Same thing."

"No. Not really, Bernard. 'I'm wanting'—you can't say that. It's bad grammar."

"Don't care."

"Bernard, please. Don't embarrass yourself in front of Babe."

Babe did her utmost to look embarrassed.

"Mam!"

"Yes, honey?"

"Can I talk to you for a second?"

"Certainly, Bernard."

Benny stalked off to the side of the stage, which was actually the lighthouse's base platform.

"Mam. This is not a good idea."

"Why's that, Bernard?"

"Because I'm a hurler, Mam. You can't make hurlers do drama. It's wrong. Like trying to shove a square peg into a round hole."

"Have you finished, Bernard?"

"Suppose."

"Good. Now go on back center stage and say the line properly."

"Ma!"

Jessica speared him with a look that would crack plate glass.

"Okay . . . Mam. I'm going. I'm going."

Benny dragged his feet back on to the stage.

"Now, off you go."

"Ah . . . How's it going? I'm here for you-know-who."

"BENNY!"

Benny swallowed. Mam had called him Benny. That had only happened twice before. Both times Benny had ended up a sorry chap. Better read the line.

He cleared his throat. "I have come to rescue the princess from the Vampire King."

Mam nodded. "Better. Georgie?"

George shook his head. "I don't know, Mother. I just didn't believe it. He's not selling the line."

"Bernard. Say it like you mean it. And face the audience!"

"What audience?"

"The audience that will be here next Saturday morning. Including Dad, your Grandfather, Jerry, Clipper, and every one of your little friends that we can get hold of."

"Oh goodie!" said Georgie.

"Oh God!" said his older brother.

Benny was in hell. And if he wasn't, then he'd rather be. His life had been ripped apart and reassembled by two drama-crazed women. A play! A play, if you don't mind! Benny couldn't believe it. Not only did he have to read outside school hours, but he had to learn words by heart. It was a disgrace. No boy should have to put up with it. Benny would have written a letter to the European Court of Human Rights, if that hadn't meant writing as well as reading.

And not only were there lines to learn, there were songs too. Georgie had oh so cleverly adapted some of the classics to fit in with the vampire theme. There was "Blood Glorious Blood" and "There Is Nothing Like a Vein," not to mention "Can You Steal My Blood Tonight?" It was ridiculous. And that wasn't even the worst of it. There were costumes, too, and makeup! Makeup? Why didn't he just hang a sign around his neck saying: Excommunicate me from the male species forever. Benny envisioned yet another tombstone for himself. This one read: *Here lies Bernard Shaw. Allowed his Mam to plaster him with makeup for a play outside school hours. Also won Guinness Player of the Championship for hurling three times, but this was overshadowed by the specter of lip gloss.* Benny shuddered. Was there no one he could turn to for help?

Babe was no use to him, that was for sure. She was too busy finding herself. The little tomboy was blooming under Jessica's tutelage and was becoming increasingly girlie every day. She had found to her amazement that she actually liked this acting thing. She could be a townie type of girl and not feel mortified, because it wasn't her being the townie girl, it was her character. This, Babe knew, was a very dodgy argument, so she tried not to dwell on it too much. And the costume was just so . . . pretty. All lace and gauze. Not the sort of thing Babe would usually wear, but definitely something the princess might throw on for a palace ball.

Babe also discovered that Georgie wasn't the Antichrist that Benny portrayed him as. He wasn't a bad little guy, actually. A bit on the thinky side, but, sure, he was useless at sport, so what option had he?

Rehearsals went on all week in preparation for the weekend's performance. At Babe's suggestion, Benny had reluctantly agreed to stockpile their lures for a big killing on the August bank-holiday weekend. This would allow them more rehearsal time, plus the place would be thronged on the Sunday. More rehearsal time was not a plus in Benny's opinion. Anything that took a healthy young male away from sport and in the direction of the written word was inherently evil. Unfortunately, Benny's opinions on just about any subject were being shared by fewer and fewer people these days.

Dress rehearsal on Friday afternoon. Full costume, makeup—and one other thing.

"We have to do the kiss today," said Jessica firmly.

"Mam!"

"Bernard. You're on tomorrow. It's your last chance for a practice run."

"Mam. Can we not cut that bit?"

"No. The prince has to kiss the princess. It's traditional."

"That's another thing, Mam. Prince Percival? Can't I have a cool sort of name?"

Jessica arched an eyebrow. "Like what, for example?"

"I don't know. Prince Brainbiter or something."

"No, Bernard. Now, let's get on. Babe, are you ready, dear?"

"Just ready," called Babe, applying another layer of lipstick.

Benny groaned. His friend was lost to him forever.

"Good. So, from the end of 'Nothing Like a Vein' and then the kiss, okay?"

Benny tried one last plea. "Mam. Can't you see this is embarrassing for Babe?"

Jessica threw down her clipboard. "Oh, for goodness' sake, Bernard! It's a little peck on the cheek!" She grabbed Georgie by the head and kissed him soundly. "There, that wasn't so bad!" Mam marched to the platform and kissed Benny on the forehead. "Is anyone embarrassed? No."

To complete the demonstration, Jessica gave Babe a hug and a kiss. "Are you all right, honey?"

Babe nodded, giggling.

"Not traumatized are you?"

"No."

Jessica turned on Benny, hands on hips. "What message are you sending here, Bernard? What's Babe supposed to think when you won't even kiss her on the cheek?"

Benny swallowed. Babe was giving him a bit of an evil eye. "Okay. All right. Let's get it over with."

"Good boy. It'll be fun, I promise."

"Yeah, yeah," muttered Benny. "About as much fun as a poke in the eye with a sharp stick."

"What was that, Bernard?"

"Nothing."

"Good. Right, cue Vampire King's song and rescue scene."

Georgie stalked onto the platform, resplendent in cape and fangs, and launched into the final chorus of his big number.

"There are no drinks like a vein,
Your fangs you'll sink in a vein,
Nothing attracts like a vein,
Or reacts like a vein,
I would kill for a vein,
Drink my fill from a vein!"

Georgie did a little two-step before the big finish.

"There ain't a thing that's wrong with any man here,
That can't be cured by putting him near,
A long and luvverly,
Red and bubbly,
Veeeeeiiiiiiinn!"

And bow.

"Excellent, George. Now, Bernard, chin up. Nice and loud."

Benny adjusted his tinfoil crown and stepped in from the wings. "Hold it right there, Vampire King!"

Georgie froze. Just about to bite into the princess's neck. "Prince Percival! How did you get into ze Castle of Darkness?" George, in fairness to him, did a pretty decent Transylvanian accent. Though sometimes he strayed across to Pakistan.

"The Molers dug a tunnel for me."

"Ze Molers? Zey wouldn't dare!"

"Oh yes zey . . . they would. I promised them potatoes!"

At this point, you have to know the whole story or things start sounding a bit silly.

"Unfang Princess Daphne!"

Georgie advanced creepily, and for a second Benny actually felt nervous. "You haf made a grave mistake coming here, Prince Percival. Zis is ze Castle of

Darkness. Sunlight is ze only zing zat can destroy me."

Benny was glad he didn't have to do all the ze-zing-zat bit.

"Here in ze Castle of Darkness, ze sunlight never shines in ze windows. You are doomed, Prince Percival."

"That's where you're mistaken, you vampire scoundrel."

There follows a dramatic slow-motion chase around the castle, with plenty of leering and near misses. Eventually, Prince Percival pulls a mirror from under his cape and sticks it out the window. The glass reflects a passing sunray and beams it straight at the Vampire King. He dies horribly. Know-it-alls among you may point out that a mere hand mirror could not possibly outreach the shadow cast by a twelfth-century eastern European tower, unless the handle were at least two hundred feet long. To those people I say: *Get a life*.

Now was the moment of truth for Benny. Having vanquished the Vampire King, he had to free the bound Princess Daphne. Benny shuffled to where Babe was struggling with imaginary ropes. He sliced them with his cardboard sword.

"Oh, Prince Percival. You have saved me. Come hither and claim your reward." Babe stuck out her cheek.

Go on, Benny my son, Benny urged himself. Just fake it. A sly near-miss kiss with plenty of noise. Like Mam did when she'd just done her makeup. No one would know. He leaned in and kissed the air on Mam's blind side.

"Again, Bernard."

"What?"

"That was terrible. If it was up to you, the Frog Prince would still be a frog. Go on, again."

Babe's cheek was still where she'd left it. Benny gave it the quickest of pecks.

"Again, Bernard. Try not to look as if you're kissing a reptile."

"Yes, Benny," hissed Babe from the corner of her mouth.

Benny tried again. Don't think of that cheek as Babe's, he told himself. Pretend you're kissing your Ma good night.

"Perfect. Good boy. That wasn't so terrible now, was it?"

"No," admitted Benny.

"Now that you've done it once, it should be much easier tomorrow with all your friends watching."

Benny wailed internally, afraid that if he let any dismay show on his face, Babe would think he was sulking over the kiss. It wasn't that he wasn't sulking over the kiss. He was. It just wasn't the primary sulk motivator. This whole dressy-up, big girl's, tra la la, dancy prancy, let's-put-on-a-show thing was really annoying him. The kiss itself hadn't been too bad.

Clinically, it had been over so fast he'd felt nothing. He might as well have been kissing Conger. But he knew that it meant something. It was another step away from being little Benny. Part of him wanted to forget about this one-step-at-a-time thing and just jump off the ladder. But another part sort of liked little Benny, and all the things he could get away with, because he was just a kid.

Furty was mounting an operation. The secret to a successful crime, he'd decided, was preparation. That's where he'd gone wrong with the chip van. No preparation. Just a spur-of-the-moment job. If he'd been staking out that van, he'd have known that the owner slept in the cab. A stupid mistake that had cost him nine months of his life. It wouldn't happen again.

He'd initially intended to mount surveillance from the roof of the salthouse, but had discovered that there wasn't sufficient altitude. So he settled on the castle tower. From this vantage point, he had a panoramic view of the rocks, right up to Black Chan. And to the northwest he could follow the road past the tower and on to his own house. Perfect.

The odd time a pang of conscience niggled at Furty's skull, but he dismissed it. It was only right. Justice. He was only doing to those two blow-ins what they'd already done to him. Returning the favor.

The blow-ins in question were pathetically easy to keep tabs on. Every day was the same. Horatio's Bridge in the morning. Puck-about after lunch, then some playacting in the evening.

He'd never figured Shaw for one of those dressy-up types. But it was all over the village about their stupid performance on the coming Saturday.

So Furty would sit in the tower, with his old brass binoculars trained on Benny and partner. Soon all their secrets were known to him. He knew, for example, that Babe copied Benny's walk behind his back. He knew that Benny practiced his part in the play on the sly. And he knew that they cleaned and stored their lures in the workshed behind the lighthouse. That was a puzzle. How to get in there unnoticed? That whole place was lit up like a Christmas tree at night. So during the day then. When no one was around. Or maybe when everyone was around. But looking the other way.

Furty grinned to himself. They were making this too easy for him.

Benny prayed for rain. Oh God, please send a typhoon down here to cut off Dugan's Tower from the rest of the world. Or failing that, a decent bank of fog curled around the base of the lighthouse would do very nicely. But it was useless. Everyone else involved in the production was much holier than he was. And they were all praying for sun. Benny imagined God stroking his white beard, weighing up the prayers. On the one hand you had Jessica, Georgie, and Babe looking for sunshine so they could put on a play for the local children. Then you had Benny Shaw praying for a storm. Benny with a rap sheet as long as your arm, a history of falling asleep during prayers, and purely selfish motives. No contest.

So before he even opened his eyes on that Saturday of the bank-holiday weekend, Benny knew that the sun was going to be splitting the stones. And, of course, it was.

Benny had his own theory of relativity. He reckoned that time was inversely proportional to need. He didn't think in those terms exactly. Benny would never use words like inversely or proportional, in case someone might accuse him of paying attention in class. His exact words were: the slower you wanted a yoke to happen, the faster it happened. This morning was a prime example. He wanted the time before the play to drag out for an eternity, like it did when he was waiting for his pocket money. But before he knew what was going on, Babe arrived with her costume.

"Howye, partner?" she beamed.

"What are you so cheery about?"

"God almighty, Benny, you're an awful chicken. The whole thing will be over before lunch."

"Over? My life will be over. Wait till the boys see me in that get up. A cloak and tights. Deadly."

"Go on. You look very handsome."

Benny scanned the comment for sarcasm. Clean. He looked handsome? It couldn't be. Benny Shaw with his cowlick and knobbly knees. Babe was just being nice.

"Ahem?"

Benny realized that she was waiting for him to return the compliment. Her icy stare said that he'd better come up with a comment quick, of his own free will.

"You look very nice, too, pixie."

Babe beamed. "Do I? Really? Thanks, Benny."

She rustled off, a big bundle of flouncy material, to check in with the director. This was getting out of hand. First dancing, then acting, and now swapping compliments. Sincere compliments too. Something wrong here—if you told a male that he looked nice, you were obviously being sarcastic, and actually meant he looked like the inside of a horse's stomach.

Benny peeked out the slit window. People were gathering on the lawn, already. Granda had put out what seats there were, and supplemented them with benches, planks, and fish boxes. Clipper and Jerry were plonked in the front row, staring in fascination at the simple backdrop taped to the lighthouse wall. Benny noticed Paudie and the Aherns cycling up the drive. Their dads must've given them the hour off specially. There were strangers too. Weekenders just strolling in off the road. Knowing his luck, the Wexford County hurling selectors would arrive and strike him off their list forever.

"Makeup."

Benny turned to see Jessica advancing toward him, brandishing a thick greasy stick of stage makeup.

"Mam? Do we have to?"

"Yes, Bernard. We do. There's a real glare coming off that tower wall. You'll look like a ghost without a bit of number nine and five."

At this moment in time, Benny would've gladly traded places with a ghost. Anything to avoid the humiliation that awaited him.

Jessica smeared a lump of goo all over his face.

"Don't scowl, Bernard. I can't do the creases."

Benny tried to unkink his face.

"Now smile. I want to do your beard."

"Beard? No, Mam. Have a heart!"

"The prince always has a beard."

In spite of himself, Benny was intrigued by the idea. A little glimpse into the future.

"Something cool now, Mam. Not a big Grizzly Adams yoke."

Jessica smiled. "Oh, we're interested now, are we?"

She put a finger under his chin, and drew on a little

beard with a mascara brush. Benny ran to study himself in the mirror. Not bad, he thought admiringly. I am a handsome devil. No wonder the chicks dig me. He shuddered. Da was right, he was watching too much Yankee telly.

"Now, Benny. Go over your lines. Five minutes to curtain."

Curtain? What curtain? These actor types were always going on like they were in the Abbey Theatre. Curtain, wings, stage. Face facts—they were on a stone platform in front of a lighthouse.

"There's no curtain, Mam."

Jessica Shaw took her son's face in her hands. "Bernard. Give it a chance. If you don't believe it, no one else will."

Benny, not being a total gom, realized that this was a meaningful moment. The mother imparting vital information to her son. A suitable reaction was called for. He blinked once, lost focus in deep contemplation, then nodded.

"Okay, Mam. I'll give it a chance."

"Good boy. Break a leg now."

Break a leg? Actors! Shower of weirdos the lot of them. Who else would urge you to break a leg or any other limb for that matter?

"I won't be breaking a leg, Mam. No more than you did in Macbeth."

Jessica gasped. "Benny! You must never say that word in a dressing room. Never!"

Benny grinned nastily. "What word? Mac—"

"Stop it, Bernard! That's very bad luck. Now to cancel out the negative karma, you have to go outside the room, turn around three times and then come back in. Okay?"

"Sure thing, Mam. No problem."

Jessica pecked him on the cheek. "Good boy. See you at the cheese and wine reception—that'll be cheese and cola for you, naturally."

"Okey dokey."

Benny watched his mother rush off to grease up the next victim. Go outside and turn around three times? I will in me dreams! We're not a crowd of pagans, you know. He snorted. As if saying Macbeth in a dressing room could bring bad luck.

"Macbeth," he whispered. "Macbeth, Macbeth, Macbeth."

A bit dopey, in retrospect, challenging fate like that. Considering what happened. Not that theatrical spirits were responsible. It was all human error. One human in particular. Guess which one.

Things started off well enough. Georgie stalked out and did his evil-vampire-looking-for-a-princess bit, and the crowd loved it. And what a crowd. Every single village resident seemed to have turned up. Plus tourists and local clergy; there was even a farmer watching in the next field from the seat of his tractor. As far as anyone could remember, this was the first play staged in Duncade since Murt Hanrahan's 1962 tragic recreation of Strongbow's assault on Waterford. The audience fervently hoped that this play would not result in quite so much bloodshed or family vendettas.

Georgie hammed it up to the hilt. Milking the audience for as many boos as possible. So, after a verse of "Blood Glorious Blood," Babe is kidnapped and whisked off to the Castle of Darkness. Enter our hero, resplendent in tinfoil crown and flowing beard, to save his beloved. And so Benny Shaw made his debut, moping onto the stage, staring determinedly at his pointy shoes, his cheeks boiling with humiliation.

Conger chose this moment to make an appearance. The mongrel mutt somehow slipped his lead, and decided to continue the daily game of "harass the townie." He hit Benny like a cannonball, careering straight into the drop cloth. They went down, dragging the cloth with them. The audience, of course, thought this was hilarious, and nearly split their stomachs laughing. Meanwhile, Benny and Conger struggled to free themselves, and the cloth billowed like some weird two-headed ghost. Eventually, Babe trotted on and apologetically removed both cloth and hound.

Benny dragged himself vertical, straightened his sword, and continued as though nothing had happened. After all, things could only get better.

Amazingly enough, things actually did get better. The audience howled with honest laughter at every opportunity, and applauded or booed at the appropriate moments. Benny sneaked a few peeks at the first row, and was amazed to see tears of laughter streaming down Da's face. A slow glow grew inside him, and he began delivering his lines with a bit more enthusiasm. Of course it was Georgie who stole the show with his villainous posturing, but Benny didn't mind. He was content just to have nothing thrown at him.

Naturally, the kiss was the highlight. Benny felt his lips go dry seconds before the deed. Oh my God! What if he stuck to Babe's face? What if they had to pull him off, like duct tape off a hostage? He winced at the thought.

In accordance with the Shaw theory of relativity, the cue arrived with staggering speed. There was Babe with her cheek aimed at Benny's head, and there he was trying to suck down a breath of air through his pinhole windpipe.

"Come on," hissed Babe, through smiling teeth.

"Go on," whispered the vampire corpse.

"Kiss her, ye eejit," shouted some heckler from the audience.

So he did. Two steps, peck, and it was over. The crowd rose to their feet, hooting and stomping. Nothing like a nice, good-triumphs-over-evil, feel-good play, with a bit of romance thrown in. Jerry's voice boomed over the rest.

"Butterflies!" he roared enthusiastically, a tear pricking the corner of his eye. And you can't get much higher praise than that.

They took three bows, and it was only afterward that Benny realized he'd been holding hands with Babe the whole time.

He caught her eye on the third bow. Her face radiated happiness, and Benny realized that they'd lost her forever. Babe Meara was no longer just one of the lads, she was one hundred percent girl.

Later, the boys sipped cola from wine glasses.

"Not a bad cola," commented Seanie. "Nice nose, but a bit fruity for my palate."

Sean nodded. "Complements the cheese adequately."

"Easi Singles, if I'm not mistaken. Ninety-nine. A good year."

"Shut up, ye pair of half-wits," said Paudie.

Babe and Benny joined the circle. Babe was still in full costume, the gauze from her conical hat fluttering behind her. Benny had attempted to remove the make-up without a mirror, and so resembled a camouflaged Desert Storm veteran.

Paudie shook their hands formally. "Good show, lads. How on earth did you get Conger to do that?"

"Training," replied Babe. "You just have to let him know who's boss."

Seanie punched Benny on the arm. "Does this mean you'll be giving up the hurling altogether to concentrate on girls' stuff?"

"I'll concentrate on you now in a minute."

"Oh, temper! You actors are very highly strung!"

Benny and Seanie collapsed on the grass, boxing.

Paudie studied his watch. "Hmm. Ten seconds. That's a new record. Usually it takes nearly half a minute for those two to start fighting."

Babe threw a kick at Benny's leg. "Hey, townie. There's fishermen down already. We could sell a few lures on our way to the pool."

Benny disentangled himself from his grinning protagonist.

"Oh, so now you want to sell lures again. Well, it's about time."

"Give up your whining, and get the tin."

Benny rubbed the grass from his jersey and made for the shed. People were still milling around after the show. Several slapped his shoulder in congratulation. Georgie was explaining his technique to an enthralled audience. Benny gave him a thumbs up, and was instantly horrified with himself. What was going on here? Civil behavior toward his brother! Next thing they'd be giving each other goodnight kisses. He posted a memo on the wall of his brain: give Crawler a hard time tomorrow to stop him getting cocky. Not today, though. Let him have his moment of glory. He deserved it.

Benny was so busy congratulating himself on his generosity that he didn't notice the shed door was ajar until he put his fingers on the handle.

Furty was disgusted. What was going on in the world when a whole fishing village pulled up oars to go and see some townies playacting? Disgraceful. Especially after what happened with Murt Hanrahan's pageant back in 1962. There were families still feuding over that.

He trained his binoculars at Dugan's Tower. There were benches set up on the lawn. A regular little garden party. How spiffing.

Furty knew he'd have to be careful. If he was spotted at this, it'd be back to Saint Julian's for him for the rest of this year. That old Paddy Shaw coot had eyes on him like a cormorant. He could pick out a fieldmouse in a field of corn. The rest of them would be afraid of their lives to do anything. But Granda Shaw would frogmarch him off to the police station without a second thought.

He trotted down the spiral staircase, letting himself out

through the old chimney stack. No one saw him leave. There was no one to see him. They were all up gawking at their new best friends. The sun was high and hot. A few wispy clouds drifted around like sheep in a pool, but the heat would have them fried out of it by early afternoon. This place was going to be hopping with families for the day. Families with money to spend.

Someone was singing. A high unbroken voice. Probably the younger townie. What kind of an eejit was he, with his dressing up and his poems? There wasn't a sinner in the tower driveway. All up around the bend, at the foot of the lighthouse. Furty strolled up the gravel, trying to step nonchalantly. As though he was supposed to be there. As though he would actually go to a play.

The workshed was on the bend in the horseshoe lane. Perfect. Furty inched his head around the corner to make sure no one was approaching. All clear. With practiced ease, he lifted the latch and slipped into the cool shade. It was all coming back to him. The nervous sweat, the sparks in his stomach. The persistent pangs of guilt that settled over his brain like a wet blanket. Ruining his triumph.

This was actually the first crime Furty had committed since his early release. A large part of him regretted returning to this life. Breaking a promise he'd made to himself one lonely night in the dormitory. But there was no other way. Life was life. There was no point moping about all day wishing you were someone else. You had to survive, whatever way you could.

The shed brought memories flooding back. It smelled of oil and work, like Da's shed used to. The tools were shiny and sharp, all clipped neatly in their brackets or adhered to a strip-magnet. Furty was surprised to find a lump growing in his throat. He blinked rapidly, banishing this weakness to the back of his head where it belonged.

Benny had obviously been given a corner to work in. Sandpaper and silver paint were laid out on a newspaper. Wet lures hung from a cork board, and rusted ones were hooked around the rim of a can of paint thinner. A regular busy beaver. A large Tupperware container was sitting on the stool. Bingo. Furty popped the top to check its contents. Full to the brim with lures. Shone up and everything. Very considerate.

Furty stuffed the box down his jumper. He didn't touch the fixer-uppers, though. Leave them. That should sow a bit of confusion among his enemies. Get them wondering if maybe Benny didn't just leave the lure box down somewhere. Maybe they weren't stolen at all. Maybe the townie just lost them.

He opened the door a sliver. No one was looking in his direction. Too busy watching Babe Meara singing her little song. It looked like she was a princess or something, and the little fellow was a vampire, trying to talk her out of a few liters of blood. He was good, that Georgie fellow, with those teeth and that walk. You'd nearly believe he was a bloodsucker. Furty was horrified to find himself chuckling at the antics on stage. Imagine, after all this preparation, to be nabbed watching the play. He shook himself. Move it out, Furty boy. Get these up to your own house straight away. Hide the evidence.

He sidled around to the shed's blind side. The crowd was still enthralled by the fate of Princess Babe. And in all honesty, Furty wouldn't have minded seeing how the whole thing worked out. What would it be like, he wondered, to be able to just sit down and enjoy something, without the problems of life crushing any spark of youth inside you?

In seconds, Furty was out on the main road and heading for the driveway. He felt bad about stealing the lures. But he felt worse about leaving those not in the box. Not because they were worth anything, but because their presence would make Shaw's friends doubt him. And maybe even make Benny doubt himself.

"I'm telling you!" shouted Benny. "That's where I put the box! Right there!"

"You're sure?" asked Babe.

"'Course I'm sure. Right there on the bait stool. Same as every night."

"Was the door locked?"

"There is no lock. Who locks doors in Duncade? Just keep it closed so critters don't get in."

"Critters?"

"You know. Rats, badgers, Aherns. Critters."

"Oh ha ha. I'm glad you're in a joking mood, townie. Here we are, on the biggest weekend of the summer, with only a handful of lures between us."

The partners were gathered around the stool where the lures weren't. Benny could feel the questions closing in on him. He was sure he'd put the box in its place. Certain sure. He'd checked the soaking lures this morning, and the box had been here.

"Could you have left them somewhere else?"

A question too far. "No! I couldn't! You know what's happened as well as I do."

"What's that?"

"Howlin, of course! Furty Howlin. He's been saying for weeks how he's going to get us."

"I know but . . ."

"But what, Babe? It's not the first time he's broken in somewhere, is it?"

"No, but . . ."

Benny was losing his temper at this stage. "But nothing! God almighty! But what, then? But what?"

Babe took a breath. "If Furty, or someone, stole the

box, then why didn't they take all these other baits?"

Benny frowned. "I don't know. Maybe he was in a hurry."

"It'd only take two seconds."

"I don't know, I said. I don't know."

"Okay. Okay, Benny, calm down. When did you last see them?"

"This morning before the play."

"This morning?"

Benny counted to ten. "Yes. This morning. Is there an echo in this room or something?"

"Well, if it was this morning, Furty must've come in during the play."

Benny blinked. That sounded unlikely even to him. "He could have. He could have done it."

"There were loads of people here, Benny."

"I know that. Wasn't I here too?"

"So you're saying that Furty Howlin walked in here in broad daylight, with dozens of people around. And after doing all that, he didn't bother with these other lures."

"Yep. That's what I'm saying."

"Hmm."

"Hmm what?"

"Benny, are you sure . . . ?"

"Yes, I'm sure all right. Absolutely certain. And if you were really my partner, you'd believe me."

Babe chewed her lip. "Okay. I believe you. We better tell your dad."

Benny shook his head. "No. This is our problem. Get the parents involved and our summer is over. We have to handle this ourselves."

"I don't know, Benny. This is illegal stuff. How do you handle that?"

"I'll think of something."

"What sort of something?"

"Give me a chance, will you? I don't know. Not yet."

This was a big lie. Benny knew exactly what he planned to do. He planned to steal the lures back. It wasn't really stealing, anyway, because the lures were his in the first place. But the new girlie Babe might have a problem with his strategy. Something about it being illegal or highly dangerous. What was Furty going to do? Report his stolen lures stolen? Hardly.

"Well, while you're thinking about it, let's get down to Horatio's Bridge. See if we can't scare up a few baits for tomorrow night."

Benny nodded. No point letting the day go to waste. The night wouldn't be going to waste either.

Benny had a history of sneaking out. In his experience you can get away with it for a good while before the hammer drops on your skull. Generally the punishment was swift and severe. Freedom and pocket money tended to go off-line for extended periods. But this was worth the risk, Benny told himself.

Night in the country is not like night in the town. There are no comforting orange balls floating overhead. The ditches are black hulks rearing on both sides and could possibly conceal anything from a combine harvester to a drink-crazed axe murderer.

Benny slipped from his room and sneaked up the Duncade road toward the Howlin cottage. He had to struggle with himself every step of the way. It would be so easy to talk himself into turning back. There were a million perfectly acceptable reasons not to go on, all clamoring for space in his brain. He felt as though a large elastic was tethered to his belt, and every step he took increased the tension. Go back, for God's sake! It's dark. You have no proof, no plan, no chance. Furty could freak out and fire you from a cliff-top. No one would ever know. You didn't even leave a note. Go back and forget all about this ridiculous idea. Things will seem better in the morning.

But the stubborn streak in Benny would not give in. They're my lures. He stole them. I'm going to get them back. End of story.

The cottage was barely half a mile up the road, but Shaw's theory of relativity was in full effect. No matter how far he walked, the lane down to Furty's home never seemed to get any nearer. Benny had ample time to contemplate all the ways he could be killed or maimed on this illicit escapade.

He could be gored by an escaped bull. Or run over by some moonshine-sodden drunk driver. He could plummet off the roadside into some garbage dump, or an ancient electricity pole could send a loose wire curling about his body.

Then there was the supernatural. Generally Benny sneered at all things unearthly, but darkness made believers out of stronger men than him. Of course, Granda had treated him to graphic renditions of all the local spooky legends. The one that sprang most forcibly to mind now was the tale of Corporal Bradshaw, a militia man whose body was two hundred years dead, but whose spirit continued to fight the 1798 rebellion. He patrolled the lanes, whispering "Friend or foe?" and skewering you either way. Benny swallowed dryly. Suddenly every branch poking from a clump of bushes became a gleaming bayonet.

Benny only realized he'd passed the Howlins' lane when he arrived at the crossroads. He retraced his steps. At last he arrived at the road. The squat cottage could be picked out by a soft light burning in a downstairs window. They were still up. What sort of people stayed up till two in the morning? Only those up to no good. Sort of like yourself, an internal cynic reminded him.

Benny traveled the lane carefully, keeping to the grassy ridge along its center. Long puddles stretched on either side, trapping dots of starlight on their surfaces. The hedgerow curled overhead, obscuring the night sky in places. It was a jungle. Obviously no one had been near this place with a mower in years. In those old movies his Ma loved, the ivory hunter always had a machete to get through this sort of undergrowth.

Benny crept across the heavily weeded gravel to the house wall, grateful for the scrap of light leaking through the window. The whitewash was damp and mossy beneath his fingers. Soft clay poked through crumbling patches. The traditional water barrel stood at the gable end, rusted through from years of overflow.

What a dump, thought Benny. How could anyone live in a dive like this?

He edged toward the window, nerves amplifying the tiniest sound. The click of pebbles seemed like an Alpine avalanche. The curtain was actually a grocery bag strung over the old curtain rail. It was ill fitting and left plenty of peepholes. Benny peered into the Howlins' cottage. The window was open; stale cigarette smoke streamed out into the night. Moths and daddy longlegs streamed in.

The inside of the cottage was in worse repair than the grounds. Yellowed wallpaper hung in willowy strips from the walls. Tufts of foam sprang from the arms of threadbare chairs, and crusty plates overflowed from the sink onto the draining board.

The fireplace was brimming with cigarette butts and crushed cans, and looked like it hadn't felt heat in years. Beside it, an old man was slumped in a chair. One foot jittered spasmodically, his heel scraping patterns in the dust. Haunted eyes rolled in his skull, the whites visible through crescent slits. Benny saw now that the man wasn't old at all. Just worn. The man had Furty's scowl, even in sleep. It was his father.

The man was moaning. An eerie whine flowing from his lips and nose. It grew in volume, running up and down in pitch. Eventually he shocked himself awake, consciousness returning with a jolt. Furty's father bolted upright, fear widening his eyes, and then settled back into the familiar grasp of his chair.

From behind a cushion he pulled a bottle of whiskey. Benny recognized it from the one kept in the visitors' cabinet at home. He twisted the cap off and took a long swig straight from the bottle. You could almost follow the alcohol's path to his stomach, as each body part jerked in turn.

He began to cry then. Long hitched sobs with a woman's name hidden inside them. From the mantelpiece he pulled a framed photograph and crushed it to his chest. Furty's mother. Benny had heard about her accident. Everyone had.

Benny shifted his gaze to the stairs. Furty was coming

down. First came his unlaced sneakers, then an old track-suit, then a tousled sleep-moody head.

"Come on, Da," he said. "Time for bed."

Jonjo Howlin tapped the photo clumsily. "Your mother," he slurred.

"I know that, Da. Now, up we go."

His father resisted. "No. I'm here and I'm staying here. Finish me drink."

Furty grasped his father's elbow. "You can have that in the morning. Bedtime now. You're waking the cows."

"Don't care. Leave me be, boy. Not too big for a lick of the belt."

"Lick of the belt!" scoffed Furty, directing his father toward the stairs. "You're belting days are over, Da."

Jonjo pushed the photograph in his son's face. "Your mother," he muttered insistently. "Don't forget, boy."

"I won't forget, Da," sighed Furty. "Don't worry."

They disappeared up the stairs, Jonjo's feet flapping at the steps like a baby.

Benny stared after them, ashamed of himself and what his spying had revealed. What were lures compared to this? For maybe the second time in his thirteen years, Benny appreciated his own life.

These humanitarian feelings lasted for about four seconds. Then Benny spotted the lure box lying right there on the windowsill.

"I knew it!" he hissed triumphantly. "The thief!"

One grab and the box was his! He reached in slowly, feeling the house's warmth creep up his arm. His fingers scrabbled at the plastic rim. Then there was a creak on the stairs, and he whipped his arm out of the light.

Furty reappeared, descending slowly and deliberately. He wiped the smears from his mother's photograph with the hem of his sweatshirt, and placed it on the mantelpiece.

"Don't worry, Ma," he whispered with uncharacteristic tenderness. "I won't forget."

Furty sank slowly into his Da's chair, hiding his face in his hands. Tears welled between his fingers, spilling down his face. Huge sobs shook his large frame, doubling him over in the chair.

Benny drew back from the window. Time to leave. So it was a wasted journey. He didn't care. It wasn't important.

Furty had lived in this house all his life. He knew when a sound didn't belong. This old cottage made a thousand night sounds, and this wasn't one of them. There was someone, or something, in the dried-up flower bed outside the window. He sneaked a look between his fingers, just in time to see Benny Shaw's face sliding into the darkness.

Shaw? Here? Of course! He'd come looking for his lures. Furty sniffed. How long had Shaw been there, and what had he seen? Probably the whole embarrassing episode. Furty felt a cold anger building inside him, a welcome replacement for the sadness. He had no right! Coming up here spying! The townie had gone too far this time. Too far by a long shot. This was gone beyond lures now. Way beyond. That boy would have to be taught a lesson, once and for all.

But lurking beneath Furty's anger was a niggling question that he couldn't shut away. Why hadn't Benny taken the lures? They were right there. He couldn't have missed them. So why hadn't he grabbed them? Furty shook his head. There was no point in trying to make sense out of townies. Square peg in a round hole.

Granda was waiting for Benny on the bottom step.

"Evening, Bosun," he said, his voice floating from the blackness.

Benny nearly hopped out of his shoes. "Granda?"

"The one and only."

A match flared around Granda's cigarette. For a moment Benny saw Paddy Shaw's mouth. It wasn't smiling. "Well?"

"Well, what?"

"Fine. I'll just get yer Da."

Benny stomach lurched. "No, Granda, wait. I was up at Furty's."

"Were you, now? Did you see what you needed to see?"

Benny nodded. "More. A whole heap more."

Granda sighed. "You got an eyeful of Jonjo so?"

"Yes."

"Well, maybe you can understand Furty a bit better now?"

"'Suppose."

Paddy Shaw grasped his grandson's arm. "You're in dangerous waters here, Benny. Do you understand?"

Benny nodded.

"Now, if you tell me that's the end of it, then I'll believe you. But if you keep up this messing with Furty, everybody's going to get involved."

"That's it, Granda. No more messing with Furty. I've had it."

"Good. I'm glad to hear it. Now, off to bed with you. Have a good rest, because Monday you start painting the bottom ring."

Benny opened his mouth to object, then thought better of it. A day's painting was a small price to pay for Granda's silence.

9

BLACK CHAN

Things were heating up for the regatta. Swarthy-looking fellows set up concessions on the quay. There was a bric-a-brac stall, darts and a curious looking circular pool, which turned out to be a duck race. The idea being that you bet on which plastic duck would cross the finish line first. A notion so ludicrous that it was bound to make a fortune.

Families descended on Duncade from all over the county. And, for one day only, they were tolerated by the gruff fishermen. Children competed in the greasy pole competition, swimming races, and canoeing. Needless to say, none of the local kids would set so much as a little toe in the water, having seen what was pumped and poured in there every day. But visiting children seemed happy enough, even when they emerged from the water plastered with rainbow patterns of floating diesel.

Benny was not exactly brimming with the holiday

spirit. In the light of day, he was regretting his decision to leave the lures behind. Furty's problems didn't excuse his actions.

"They were right there in front of me," he said, wrenching another clump of moss from the salthouse roof. "All I had to do was reach out my hand."

"You were mad going up there in the first place," said Babe. "Furty could have gone off the deep end altogether. It's only lures, Benny. We can find more."

"That's not the point, though. They were my . . . our lures." He gestured toward the crowds milling about the seafront. "Look at this lot. We could have made a fortune."

Babe held on to Conger's collar, stopping him from hurling himself off the roof. "It's just money."

"You're the one always going on about buying this and that. What about your bike? And those boots?"

"I'm fed up too, you know. I found most of those lures, remember. But this whole bait war thing is starting to scare me."

Benny started. Babe Meara scared? "You—scared? You are in your dreams."

Babe bristled. "I don't mean scared scared. I mean sort of worried. I think we should talk to your Granda."

"No!"

"All right. I was only saying."

"I'm not running home crying. That's what Furty wants. Poor little townie, boo hoo. No way."

"What then? Go back to his house?"

An image flashed through Benny's head. An old man sobbing in his armchair. "No. Too spooky. We have to do like Granda said. Adapt." Father Barty, Benny's trainer, had always said: "The best revenge is on the scoreboard." Benny never understood that until now. "We don't have to do anything to Furty," he explained. "We just have to sell more lures than him."

Babe scratched her chin. "Brilliant plan, Einstein. Except for we only have twelve manky old lures in the pouch. Not to mention the fact that we can't go diving today because there's already people on the rocks."

"I sort of have an idea."

"Oh? Don't tell me. We're just going to pull the lures out of our magic bags? I don't know, townie. I thought I had you cured of stupidity."

"All we need is about fifty lures."

"Fifty? Sure why not make it a hundred? A thousand? You've about as much chance."

Benny paused. "Not if you knew where to look."

Babe nearly screamed in frustration. "Benny! Forget it, will you? The only place you'd find fifty lures is down in . . . No!"

"Yep."

"Benny! You said yourself it's too dangerous."

"Yeah, but that was when I didn't know what I was doing. We could do it now. No problem."

The idea had a grip on Babe already. "I dunno, Benny."

"Imagine the look on Furty's face if we set up tonight."

A grin was beginning to tug at Babe's lips. She was, after all, Babe Meara. "That'd be something, all right."

"So, we're going down Black Chan?"

Babe raised her palms. "Hold on now, townie. I'm not making any promises. Not before we take a closer look."

"Come on, then."

"What—now?"

Benny shrugged. "Why not? Tide should be down in an hour or so."

"What about the black chicken?"

"Sure, that was only one of Granda's old stories. Probably robbed from some movie."

They skidded down the salthouse roof and into the meadows. You could tell by the faces on them that they were up to something forbidden. Their eyes were bright, and a waxy pallor shone beneath their sun-beaten faces. Even Conger was excited, scampering in little circles around their feet. He could smell a hunt.

Black Chan looked a lot deeper than it had yesterday.

That was always the way. Things always looked easier or softer or lower, until you were facing them yourself. At the moment, the channel resembled a giant mouth, with its row of jagged teeth guarding the entrance. Green weed streamed from between the molar rocks, and the glint of rusted engines winked through the spray.

"Wow," breathed Babe.

Benny whistled. "Long way down."

"You're not scared, are you?"

"Terrified."

"Me too."

This was the moment. All it would have taken at this point was one of them to show a hint of hesitation and they could have backed out without loss of face. But no. The pride of teenagers knows no bounds.

They climbed the barbed-wire fence and skirted the edge to what seemed the most accessible face. A typically blunt sign stood ominously at the lip of the abyss. It said, KILLED SO FAR: 36. The three was painted, but the six was stuck on over the previous unit. Underneath the statistics was a public safety caption that read: IF YOU SEE A PERSON OR PERSONS TRAPPED IN THE CHANNEL, PLEASE CALL SAINT PETER AND TELL HIM SOMEONE'S COMING. Some local wit had superimposed the second bit over the original text.

Babe swallowed. "Thirty-six killed. That's a fair old whack."

"They just put that up to scare tourists. Anyway, most of them were killed in that black chicken thing."

"That's a relief, then," said Babe dryly.

Now, all teenagers have a defective gene. It causes a minor short circuit in the brain, and is known as I Dunno Syndrome. This is because when asked why in the name of God they performed a certain act, they will invariably reply: I dunno. Thankfully the condition is temporary, but while under its influence, said teenagers believe it is possible to undertake any task, however ludicrous, because they are invincible. It was unfortunate that both Benny and Babe were at a high point in their I Dunno cycle at the time of the climb.

"Are you right, then?" asked Benny.

"After you."

Benny took a deep breath. "Okay, so. After me it is."

He looked down at his flimsy trainers. He was buying a pair of Timberlands tomorrow. Definitely. The cliff yawned below, daring him to set foot on it. Limestone slabs stood like rough tombstones, with dark crevices at their borders. There were easy parts—gentle gradients and wide fissures. But for the most part, it was sheer wall.

"Steps cut into the rock!" muttered Benny. "Ha! Thanks very much, Granda."

Turning so that his back faced the ocean, Benny began his descent. Everything seemed larger than life. The sun was hotter on his neck. The wind seemed to grow from a cooling breeze to a dangerous bluster. What the hell am I doing? he thought briefly. But then it was gone, lost in the strange thrill of the moment.

He put a foot down, then another. He was committed, nowhere to go but to the bottom.

Benny was lucky, really. He had the agility of a goat, though he'd probably prefer to be compared to something a bit nobler. He'd taken his first steps at the age of ten months, and was running before he was one. His Da secretly reckoned that this accounted for his slightly bandy stance, as his little legs hadn't been able to cope with the weight of that pudgy body. Like putting an elephant on stilts. By the time he was three, he would tear flat out along the top of the garden wall, nearly giving Jessica Shaw several coronaries. By school age, one of Benny's favorite hobbies was to climb trees with his hands in his pockets. So, for him, Black Chan was just the latest in a line of challenges against gravity.

Babe had been climbing every day of her life for years. She was built for it. Short and wiry, with a low center of gravity. Her thin fingers could slip into the tiniest of cracks and anchor her to a rock face like a limpet. Of course having a pair of Timberlands, the finest rock shoe known to man, didn't hurt.

They descended slowly, kicking each toehold thoroughly before trusting to it. There was no banter or comments. All available energy was devoted to getting down. Conger was not experiencing the same degree of difficulty as the humans. Actually, he wasn't experiencing any difficulty whatsoever. What was only the narrowest of ledges to Babe and Benny was a virtual platform to the diminutive mutt. He hopped easily from level to level, yipping impatiently for the other pair to hurry up.

The final third of the descent was the hardest. Below the tideline now, it was harder to find grips in the worn rock. Slime was spreading its fuzz along the cliff face, hiding in the recesses of any crack, waiting to dislodge a careless foot. Benny's fingers were stiffening, and cracks of pain spread across his back. He was stretching muscles rarely used in daily activity. Even his toes were sore, bent back through the flimsy material of his trainers. Eventually, with eight feet to go, he couldn't find a single foothold.

"I'm stuck!" he shouted to Babe.

"Jump, then!"

"Jump?"

"What are you going to do? Go back up?"

She was right. They had no choice. Benny flattened himself along the slick rock face and slid down its surface. He landed on the loose shale, bending his knees with the impact. In seconds, Babe was standing beside him, brushing the dust from her jeans.

"That wasn't half as bad as I thought," commented Benny.

Babe leaned against the cliff wall, the color gradually returning to her face. "No. A cakewalk. Let's do it again tomorrow."

Benny shuddered. This was a one-time-only deal as far as he was concerned. And if Granda ever found out about it, it would probably be the last time he'd set foot on the rocks for the whole summer.

"Well, I just hope it was worth it."

Black Chan looked a lot different from this angle. Like being inside a stone cauldron. The cliff teetered above them, seeming almost ready to collapse.

"Did we just climb down that?" croaked Benny.

"Yep."

The inlet itself was dark and untouched by the sun. Normal plant life could not survive here. It would either be blasted by the saltwater, or starved by the darkness. Jagged caves retreated into total blackness from the rock face.

"Tell you where I'm not going," said Babe, nodding at the caves.

"You don't have to tell me," replied Benny. "I'm not going there either."

"I'm glad that's decided. I would've hated to leave your townie corpse to rot in one of those black holes."

"Thanks very much."

"Welcome."

It is a testament to the recuperative power of teenagers that Benny and Babe slipped so quickly into their usual banter. They had already recovered from the stress of the descent. Your average adult would be having nightmares for months after an ordeal like that, and would possibly need therapy. But to Benny and Babe, it was far less stressful than, say, having to kiss someone on the cheek in front of all your friends.

They hurried past the shade line into the sunlight, eager for the comfort of familiar sights and smells. Even the clumps of purple thrift were a welcome addition to the bleak scenery. They were at home now. This was their business.

Flat slabs gave way to crushed pebbles, and the stones in turn yielded to thick shanks of weed. The partners skipped across protruding rocks until they reached the Chan's teeth.

Babe patted a jagged rock the size of a mailbox.

"These chaps are what'll make our money for us," she explained. "They're like a giant sieve. Anything that's pushed inland by the currents gets jammed in here."

The teeth ran across the entire inlet in a rough semi-circle. A mini mountain range. Outside, the ocean slapped at the base of the pillars, but it was too low to breast the barricade. Benny peered between two of the teeth. A thick layer of scum and rot had built up over the years. Shards of metal and wood protruded from the silt. The stink was horrendous.

Benny's nose wrinkled. "Oh! Worse than a barn full of farmers."

"Too much for your delicate townie nostrils, is it?"

"No. I'm used to it at this stage. What with you crowd spreading slurry all the time."

Babe punched him. "I do not personally spread slurry."

"Whatever. Right, let's get a move on and get out of here."

Babe nodded. "You go starboard. I'll go port."

Benny frowned. "Starboard . . . Don't tell me. That'd be . . ."

"Right, you ignoramus. You go right."

"I knew that."

"Sure, townie. 'Course you did, just like you knew what a Vee Bee was."

"Bring that up, why don't you!"

The ground immediately inside the teeth was dotted with rock pools and ankle-twisting holes. Benny kept to sundried rocks on his trek to the right cliff face. On his way, he yanked a twisted metal bar from under a rock. If you're going to clean teeth, you need a toothpick.

The vee between the first two columns was piled with

gunk. A seagull perched on top, gripping the weed with its webbed claws. This was a big gull. Big and evil looking. Like that devil crow in that movie. It gave Benny the evil eye.

What is it with me and animals? he thought, waving the iron bar feebly at the seagull. If the bird could have chuckled derisively, it would have. Instead, it settled for an unimpressed screech, and didn't budge so much as a wing. I'll come back to that one, Benny decided, shuffling on to the next rock.

If there was a more disgusting job, then Benny would like to see it. Or rather he wouldn't like to see it. This was quite revolting enough for him. First the stench assaulted your nostrils. Then when you scraped away the dried crust, a whole jumble of new aromas was released. Rotting fish, split rubbish bags, dead seagulls, diesel-soaked weed, to name just a few.

Benny dug his pick into the center of the pile and raked it through. The pulpy mass fell to the rocks with a plop.

He held his breath and knelt beside it. Even at first glance he could see several metallic glints in the pile. Screwing up his courage, he plunged his hands into the foul mass. It felt worse than it looked. Slimy, slippery, with hard bits and things that wriggled. Fighting the urge to chicken out, Benny grabbed one of the shiny bits, and pulled. It was a lure. A jumbo German! On his very first try.

"Got one!" he shouted, waving his prize.

Babe was peeling strands of something sludgy from a spooner. "Me too. The place is crawling with them."

Crawling, thought Benny. That's not all it's crawling with. But he knew he couldn't whine. Not out loud at any rate. Because the whole thing had been his idea.

Benny stripped off his sweatshirt and tied it around his face. The shirt, he reckoned, didn't smell quite as offensive as the goo they were sifting through.

Furty was back on surveillance duty. As far as he was concerned, the conflict with Shaw had escalated to all-out war. And because preparation had paid off handsomely with the last little caper, he would watch them a while before deciding how best to extract revenge.

Furty was in an especially foul mood today. He hated the regatta, with all those smarmy families swarming around, sucking ice pops like they didn't have a problem in the world. It was all fake. Just an act to show everyone how happy they were. As soon as they were back in the car, Daddy would be shouting at his kids to shut up.

He couldn't haul in his trap either with all those people on the rocks. He couldn't even hunt the water's edge for legitimately snagged lures. True, he'd boasted that hunting was for kids. But that had been all talk. In reality, he needed every lure he could get if he was to make it out of Duncade this summer.

Furty needed even more lures than Benny and Babe, because he had a middleman. The tackle-shop owner had agreed to give him a good price on whatever he came up with. Furty could have done the selling himself, but he didn't even like talking to these townies, never mind begging them for money.

Furty shook the old binoculars, trying to threaten a better focus out of them. There they were, the two love birds, heading across the bank. They'd be holding hands next. What were they up to now? Something stupid, no doubt. Maybe something that he could take advantage of.

They wouldn't be diving at Horatio's Bridge today, not with all the stray hooks flying in there. Although, the way some of those townies aimed their lures, maybe the water was the safest place to be. So what were they doing? A personal service. Selling on the move. Why did they pass the busiest rocks then?

Furty glowered at the distant pair. He didn't like this. Not knowing. Maybe those two were just clever enough to pull off some stunt. Especially if they'd gone to that crusty old Paddy Shaw for advice. That chap had more tricks up his sleeve than a roomful of magicians. There was a chance in a million that they could somehow beat him, but with his family's luck, that's about all they'd need.

They were going over the fence! Unbelievable! Surely they weren't thick enough to . . . No! No, they were thick enough. They were actually going down into Black Chan. Furty grinned. They were dumber than they looked. Actually, they were exactly as dumb as they looked. He smiled again, enjoying his own wit. He'd have to remember that one to tell at their funeral.

Furty inched down from the mossy roof. This definitely merited a closer look.

Benny reared back in disgust. The hollow sockets of a skull were staring back at him from between two columns. A hermit crab clicked around in an eye hole.

"God almighty!" he cried, feeling his breakfast threatening to rejoin the outside world.

"Seal," said Babe.

"What?"

"It's a seal. Look. Flippers."

Benny looked. Only the head had been completely stripped. The remains of a flipper hung limply from a few strings of fur.

"This is charming. I love this job."

"Your idea, townie. I'd hate to see you in a slaughter-house."

"So would I."

Benny tried to drag the subject away from his wimpishness. "The tide is fairly low still."

Babe nodded thoughtfully. "I know. We're here a

good hour and a half now, and no move on the tideline."

Benny shrugged. "Ah well. You know what they say. A watched pot never boils."

"A watched kettle."

"Pot."

"Kettle."

"For God's sake, pixie, you'd argue over anything. Pot."

Babe solved the argument with a deadarm.

Benny rubbed his shoulder. "We'd better get on with it before the water does rise. I don't want to be here when that chicken arrives."

"Me neither. We'll give it another half hour. Then we better clear out."

Benny nodded. No point in taking risks. They already had enough lures to set up shop tonight. He eyed the seal skull warily; the skull returned his gaze. He could probably poke his bar into the eye socket, and whip the head out of there. Then again, maybe not. Benny walked carefully back to the first column. Maybe the devil seagull was gone.

Furty was peering down into Black Chan. He took the binoculars away from his face to confirm what the lenses were telling him. Yep. They were still there, lure hunting in the teeth by the looks of it. He snorted incredulously. Why didn't they just hurl themselves from the top of the castle? He was surprised at Shaw really. Acting like some stupid tourist. Didn't they see the sign? It was blunt enough, that was for sure.

The problem with the Chan wasn't getting down there. The cliffs were handy enough. Furty himself had been down there on many occasions. The problem was the effect the rock columns had on the tide. The gaps in the teeth were clogged with all sorts of junk, and acted as a natural dam. The water was held at bay behind the wall, giving the impression of low tide. Then suddenly, in a matter of minutes, the water would come over the top, popping many of the blocked gaps. Once a wave came in, it was trapped, unable to retreat. The Chan filled like a bowl under the tap. The confined current transformed into vicious undertow, whipping the legs from anything that was standing. In this case the blow-ins and pet.

There was one more problem. The climb back up. Getting down was easy, but the punishing tide had long since battered any handholds for the last ten feet or so. If you wanted to get out of Black Chan, you'd better have left a rope tied off at the last grip. If not, the only way to escape was by sea. And, as far as Furty could see, they hadn't brought a boat. You could shout all you wanted, no one was going to hear you at the bottom of Black Chan. After all, who'd be stupid enough to ignore the sign and climb the fence?

He stuffed his binoculars in his coat pocket. If a person had a boat and was to arrive at the mouth of the Chan, then that person would be in a strong bargaining position. Furty set off across the bank at a run. He didn't actually have a boat himself, but he knew a man who did. A man who shouldn't be around for a while.

There was a red-eye jammed right down between two of the jagged teeth. Benny had spent the past ten minutes hacking away at the crud to get at it, and there was no way he was giving up now.

"You might as well surrender," he grunted at the piece of metal. "Benny Shaw leaves nothing behind."

"What?" said Babe.

"Nothing. Just threatening a lure."

"Oh."

Babe returned to her work, his answer a perfectly acceptable one to her.

Benny was a man possessed. This would be the biggest haul ever brought back from one trip. He already had thirty-two lures, not to mention an old watch, two smooth coins (hopefully gold), and an ancient biscuit tin. Ideal for storing the day's catch. Benny could see Timberland boots and a Leatherman knife in his immediate future. This would be a real kick in the teeth for Howlin. And they weren't finished yet.

There was a big weed-covered rock separating him from his red-eye. Benny jammed the bar underneath and put his weight on it. It didn't budge. "No way, rock!"

"What?"

"Just threatening the rock."

"Oh. Okay."

Benny walked along the bar, and bounced on its tip. The bar screeched and bent. The stone ground and groaned. And popped! It bounced and rolled, sending the lure clinking into a rock pool.

"Yes!" shouted Benny gleefully, reaching for the red-eye. His hand froze half-way. Water was pouring through the gap where the rock had been anchored. A lot of water.

Benny frowned. "Babe!"

His partner's head appeared from the base of a lime-stone monolith. "What is it now, townie? Another seal scaring you?"

"No," replied Benny. "I think we'd better go. Right now."

The village was crawling with visitors. Betting on rubber ducks, for God's sake! Furty sidled along the dock, trying to calm his body down after the run. His heart was beating so hard he could feel it in his ears, and he was certain that his face must be as red as an apple.

Clipper's punt was right where it should be, tethered to

the side of his trawler. Clipper was fishing the cod grounds this last few weeks, so he'd be tucked up in bed until the evening tide. Perfect. Furty would have the little boat back before it was ever missed. And if, by some stroke of misfortune, he was caught, he could claim it was an emergency, and he was only trying to help. Furty grinned. This surveillance bit was really paying off. He'd have his flat in Dublin in no time.

There were brats on the steps fishing for crawlies. Furty resisted the temptation to accidentally boot a couple of them into the dock. This was not the time to draw attention to yourself. The boats were tied up three deep at the wall. Furty stepped out over the Mary Jane, the Mary Eileen and the Mary Rose, before dropping into the punt. The fiberglass craft swayed erratically beneath him. Furty let his knees go loose and went with the sway. Landlubbers stiffened automatically, absorbing the shock. Mariners didn't try to fight the sea. Furty realized that this was his first time in a boat since his release. He hadn't even known he'd missed it.

He pulled the plastic cover from the outboard. Five horsepower only. Not exactly jet powered, but it would have to do. Furty primed it and wound the cord around the pull starter. It caught first time. Fair play to Clipper, he kept his engines in good shape. Furty cast off the bowline and took in the fenders. Then, twisting the throttle wide, he swung the little craft in a tight arc and motored up the coast.

Clipper and Jerry were putting a few bob on the duck race. Clipper had sworn to his wife that he'd stay away from the stall, after the scalding he got last year. Straight home to bed, he'd promised. But how could you resist those little fellows, with their cute red bills, doing their best to get around the course?

Just one bet, he told himself. Just one. A pound on that plucky number nine with the plaster on his wing. The owner took his coin, and started the little compressor under the stall.

As it turned out, number nine had a plaster on its wing because of a leak. It sank halfway through the second lap. Clipper complained bitterly, but to no avail. He reckoned he'd chance one more bet, to break even.

An hour later, Clipper was still trying to break even. He was twenty quid down, and seemed to be jinxing every duck he picked. He saw them differently now. Their cuteness seemed somehow evil. Their chirpy grins transformed to smarmy sneers. Devil ducks.

Jerry Bent loomed over his shoulder checking the form. He wouldn't spend a penny himself, not Jerry. But he was quite happy distracting a person with his one-word advice.

Clipper could feel the gambling fever taking hold of

him. "Jerry. Would you shut up with your butterflies. I'm trying to concentrate."

"Butterflies," sniffed Jerry, highly insulted.

"Well, excuse me, Mr. Touchy. But I'm trying to win back the shopping money here."

Jerry knew when he wasn't wanted. He strolled over to the bench for a few warm-up spits before today's competition. One more victory and he got a perpetual trophy. The wall was already lined with hopefuls, launching long streamers into the shallows. A couple of good contenders too. A young lady from Fethard-on-sea was landing them consistently beyond the ten-meter marker.

Jerry's gaze wandered across to the outside dock. The Aherns were in, the stink rising off their craft in waves. And there was Clipper's boat, the *Mary Rose*. Immaculate, as usual. Jerry eyes stopped roving. Someone was in Clipper's punt. It was that blackguard Furty Howlin. What was that good-for-nothing after? He was casting off! This was awful altogether! That thief, making off with Clipper's boat in broad daylight!

Jerry rushed back to the duck stall. Clipper was in the throes of urging his duck on. "Come on, baby. Come on, you good thing!"

Jerry grabbed his elbow. "Butterflies," he said urgently.

"Not now, Jerry," snapped Clipper, pulling his arm away. "I'm doing something here."

Jerry shook him again. "Butterflies. Butterflies!"

"Go away!"

Jerry sighed. This was like watching an episode of *Scooby Doo*. He grabbed Clipper in his bearlike arms, and hauled him bodily to the quay wall.

"BUTTERFLIES!" he said, pointing his captive's face at the outside dock. They were just in time to see the punt swerve into open sea.

"What the hell!" swore Clipper. "That thieving . . . Come on, I'm not gonna sit around here with him gallivanting around in me punt."

"Butterflies?" asked Jerry.

"We're going after him, of course. He won't out run the big boat in that little yoke."

They ran around the quay wall, stopping only to untie thick ropes from the ancient brass bollards. In seconds, Clipper had fired up the *Mary Rose*'s diesel engines. With twenty-five horsepower under the hood, it should only be a matter of minutes before they caught up with Furty. And then, there'd be hell to pay.

Benny was searching the rock face for handholds. There were none. The sea had ground the stone's surface down to a shiny veneer. He edged along the cliff, running his hands over the smooth limestone. Nothing. All flatness and gentle ripples.

"Anything?" he shouted across at Babe.

"Nope. Nothing you could get so much as a little finger into."

They were in trouble. Major trouble. The water was rising at a ferocious rate. Spurting through the stones, tearing away chunks of silt. Every chunk increased the volume of flow.

It was hard to believe that they were actually in danger, that something bad could happen to them. That only happened on the news. To children they'd never heard of. Children who disobeyed public warnings. Benny realized that if they were drowned, the television would brand them as a pair of eejits, who died through their own stupidity.

"What about the caves?"

Babe frowned. "No. We'd just get trapped. We have to get as high as we can. Try to wait it out."

"Maybe someone will come looking for us?"

"Not for me. Ma is used to me being out lure hunting for hours."

It was true, Benny realized. Everyone would naturally assume they were out searching the rocks. Not this particular rock, though.

Another blockage popped. A jet of water sprayed the two teenagers, rolling them into the shallows. It was like getting a blow from a water cannon. Spluttering and choking, they struggled to their feet. Benny realized, with a shock, that the entire area was under water. They were running out of time.

"Quick!" he shouted above the roar of the deluge. "Up on the highest tooth!"

They waded through the churning water. The under-tow dragged at their legs with fluid fingers, trying to topple them into the surf. Babe stuffed Conger under her arm.

"That one. Look!"

One flat-topped column had ample footholds on its sheltered side. It was at least ten feet high. Maybe just high enough to keep their feet out of the water.

Benny grabbed Conger by the collar. "Right. You first. I'll hand up the lures to you."

"Conger first."

"Yeah. Of course. Conger first."

"Forget the lures, Benny. This is serious."

"No way, Babe. I didn't come down here for nothing."

"Benny!"

"There's no time for arguing. Go on up!"

Babe took a breath to complain, but thought better of it. Benny had that look on his face. The same one Conger got when he was chewing on an eel. Babe wiped the spray from her face and reached for the first handhold. Benny boosted her from below, and in seconds she was straddling the pillar.

"Okay," she yelled. "Gimme the dog."

Benny put one hand under Conger's rump and heaved him into the air. The mutt attempted a vertical run, his claws clicking on the slick rock. Babe grabbed a handful of hackle fur, and dragged Conger to dry ground.

"Now these," said Benny, firing up the lure box.

"Got 'em," grunted Babe, stowing the box under her arm.

Benny stuck his foot in a crevice, and launched himself upward. The rock was an easy climb, dotted with cracks and shelves. Soon he was wedged on the summit, icy water soaking through the seat of his pants.

"You take me to the most romantic places," muttered Babe.

"Only the best for my partner."

This was definitely a case of laughter to hide tears. There was nothing the two would have liked better than to have a big sob in the arms of their mothers. But they couldn't admit that. Even in the face of mortal danger, it was important to maintain coolness. Especially with members of the opposite sex.

They sat huddled together, spray drifting down on them in a haze. The water rose steadily, bubbling and fizzing around the base of the column. Strands of weed spun in the currents, then were snapped under by the vicious undertow.

"I'd say we're okay here," chattered Benny through

clicking teeth. "The tide will hardly make it up this far."

Babe squinted down the length of the column. "I dunno. There's no tide line. It'll be touch and go."

"Maybe some boat will pass by and see us."

"Doubt it. You couldn't catch a cold in these waters. Not with all the whirlpools. No lobster trains up here either. No one goes past Katy's Ribbon. No sandy seabed."

Benny moaned. "That's just great, now, isn't it?"

It seemed pretty bleak. Stranded on a stone column, with the tide inching up the sides. All they could do was pray that the waters would subside before washing them from their perch. The best they could hope for was to be stuck here for a couple of hours until the ocean subsided.

It's funny what runs through your mind at a time like that. All Benny could think about was that his Ma would kill him for missing dinner.

It was a bit choppy in the open sea, but Furty put the punt's nose straight into it and then cut inland for a while. Once he rounded Katy's Ribbon, any shelter the rocks had been providing was blown away. The waves had white horses on their crests, which was a bad sign. Nothing that would bother a trawler, but certainly enough to flip a punt in the wrong hands.

Furty shifted his bulk to the port gunwale, steadying the

small craft. The lip of Black Chan was sneaking into view. The teeth were acting as vaporizers, floating a low fog around the mouth of the Chan. Furty squinted into the haze. Most of the columns were submerged, whirlpools spinning around their bases. The obstructions between the teeth caused irregular blowholes to spout up erratically. There was no sign of the two partners.

Furty shook the spray from his hair, twisting the throttle open to the max. He'd have to go in closer.

"Listen!" said Babe. "Is that an engine?"

They were standing on the pillar now, waves cresting the flat top of their perch. A spitting blowhole erupting with every push of the tide. Conger was struggling frantically in Babe's arms. Babe clamped his jaws shut with her hand.

"Shhh, boy. Quiet!"

Benny listened, imagining the regular beats of an engine hidden in the natural hubbub. "I don't know. Maybe."

A wave surged over their ankles, dragging Benny's feet from under him. He collapsed on the rock, chest scraping the barnacled stone.

"Benny!" screamed Babe, the repressed tears suddenly streaming down her cheeks.

Benny opened his mouth to reassure her, but a gallon

of salt water took the opportunity to cram itself down his throat.

Babe jammed Conger between her knees and reached to help her partner. "Let go of that tin, Benny!"

Unable to speak, Benny shook his head. No way.

"Let it go!"

Benny coughed up a lungful of slop. "No. Never."

Babe grabbed her partner by the hair and dragged him on to the rock. "You stupid townie! Are you trying to kill yourself?"

Benny coughed up the remainder of his stomach's contents. What was she talking about? He had to save the lures, didn't he? He inched delicately to his feet, and wrapped his arms around Babe. They were beyond embarrassment, the seriousness of their plight rammed home by Benny's close call.

Furty spotted them. Stranded on the high rock with the sea whipping itself into a frenzy all around them. They were dead meat for sure. All thoughts of lures and revenge evaporated from Furty's mind. This was serious. These weren't his enemies now, they were just two bedraggled kids in mortal fear for their lives.

Furty studied the run of the water. He could feel the tide dragging at the keel, and he knew that those little whirlpools would spin the punt like a spider in a drain. His approach had to be just right, and even then there'd only be seconds to take those two morons on board. Furty rocked the punt experimentally. There'd be more ballast with extra bodies. But more weight too, maybe too much for the little five-horsepower.

No time to talk himself out of it. He had to go in now, before Benny and Babe were dragged off the rock and hurled on to the cliff wall. Furty shifted to the center of the boat, stretching back to control the tiller. The boat was more evenly balanced now. He'd have to reverse in, nudging the throttle to keep off the reef. If his judgment wasn't spot on, there'd be three people on that rock.

Babe parted her drenched hair, wringing it out behind her head. "It's Furty," she shouted, pointing at the approaching punt.

Benny peered through the spray. "Furty? What the hell does he want?"

"Who cares? We can fight about it later."

Benny hugged the tin to his chest. Afterward, when asked, he could never explain what took hold of his brain in those traumatic moments. Some kind of stubborn selfishness. If he could save the lures, then everything else would be all right.

"He's only after our lures. I know him."

"Forget those stupid lures!" screamed Babe, her voice

tinged with more than a touch of hysteria. The water was lapping at their knees now, every surge threatening to sweep them into the whirlpools. Babe was desperately trying to hold on to her wriggling pet, and here was Benny wasting energy on those stupid lures. "Who cares about the lures? I just want to get out of here alive."

Benny didn't answer. He glared suspiciously at the boat, and pulled the tin closer to his chest.

"Furty!" yelled Babe. "Over here!"

The shadowy figure waved, raising a finger.

"He's coming," breathed Babe, relief flooding her face. "Thank God."

"We'll see," said Benny, through gritted teeth.

Furty inched in backward, teasing spurts of power from the engine.

"Come on!" he shouted at the shivering pair.

Benny shook his head. "No. It's some sort of trick to get the lures."

"Jump!"

"No!"

Babe was incredulous. "Benny, please!"

Furty reached out his free hand. "Meara! Let's go. Quickly."

Babe cast one more beseeching look at her partner. "Benny?"

His face remained stony.

"Come on! I don't have all day."

Babe jumped. It was only a few feet but the angle was awkward. The outboard was blocking the stern, and the keel bobbed in the swell. She made it. Barely. Her fingers scrabbling over the gunwale. Furty grabbed her by the scruff and dumped her into the bilges. She came up spitting diesel.

"Benny," she coughed. "Jump!"

Then Babe noticed that Conger wasn't under her arm anymore. She'd lost him in the confusion. "Oh my God! Conger!"

Benny spotted the little dog, gamely paddling through the currents. He hadn't a prayer. The tide dragged him effortlessly toward the rocks.

"Here's a big one!" roared Furty over his shoulder.

He tried to power out of danger, but left it a moment too late. The wave whacked their craft into one of the limestone pillars. Not a serious blow. Not enough to sink them. But certainly enough to bend the prop blades like rose petals. Cursing mightily, Furty grabbed an oar from the spur and tried to pole them off the rocks.

"Where's Conger?" cried Babe.

Benny scanned the black surface. No sign. But he could hear something, a sharp howling cutting through the surf's roar.

"There, look!"

Benny followed Babe's gaze. Conger was pinned between the rocks, jammed in the wreckage of an ancient engine. He was wriggling feebly, obviously hurt.

"Benny!"

It seemed to Benny as though he was caught in a whirlwind. Too many things were happening all at once. When he tried to focus on something, it slipped away to be replaced by another crisis. Now Conger was trapped, successive waves submerging his head. Babe and Furty were drifting down along the teeth, further away from him. He was stranded without help in sight. And he had a fortune in lures under his arm, with little hope of selling them.

"Benny!"

Babe's scream snapped him out of his daze. He waited for a lull between waves and then lay flat on the rock.

"Conger! Here, boy."

The dog stretched his head back, tendons like wire under his fur. A wave broke over them, driving the wind from Benny's chest. It left him battered and breathless. He inched down further, only his legs anchoring him to the rock.

"Come on, boy. Come on."

His fingertips touched Conger's ears. Just a few more inches and he'd have the collar. Another wave. It fell like a hammer, driving liquid wedges between Benny and the rock. It was worse for the dog. His one eye was growing dull, his paws hung limp and useless. Benny made one last lunge. His scrabbling fingers closed around the dog collar. He yanked hard. No time left to worry about whatever Conger's injuries might be. The effort freed the dog, but also popped the lure tin out from under his chest.

"No!" he groaned. Not after all this.

Furty was putting his weight behind an oar, propelling them along the Chan's teeth. Miraculously, they managed to draw abreast.

"Benny," he howled. "Hurry."

Babe was perched in the prow, her arms stretched toward boy and dog. Benny cradled the shivering mutt in his arms. Blood was flowing from a long gash in its side.

"Catch!" he roared into the wind.

Babe nodded, flexing her fingers. Benny swung twice and let go. Conger sailed through the air, slipping through Babe's fingers and landing with a thud on the deck. Furty gently placed a boot on his back to pin him down.

Babe almost smiled. "Now you, Benny. Now you."

Benny shook his head. He could still see the lures. They were so close. Just above the spot where Conger had been. All he had to do was lean down. Just a second. That's all it would take.

"The tin," he shouted, pointing. "Just one second."

"No, Shaw!" protested Furty. "I can't hold her."

Babe buried her face in her hands, unable to watch.

Benny prostrated himself again, stretching his arm almost out of its socket. He would have reached them, too. Easily. His fingers were already closing on the metal, when the wave came. It wasn't a big wave. Not heightwise. It was more like a freight train. Fast and low. The wave snapped Furty's oar and sent the halves spinning into the Chan. It lifted Benny and hurled him into the surf. He felt it flow beneath his clothes, billowing them like a clown suit. He was rolled to the shallows, dragging his chest along the gravel. Then for a finale, the wave dragged him back to his point of origin and entangled him in the wrecked engine.

The machinery picked that precise moment, after decades of immobility, to surrender to the power of the sea. It groaned and screeched, the sound burrowing into the nightmare section of Benny's brain. Then, pendulously it toppled, tumbling slowly from its niche. On its way to a watery grave, a flat face of the engine connected with Benny's leg. There was a crunch, like a walnut under a mallet. Oops, thought Benny, deep in shock and feeling absolutely no pain whatsoever. That's not just one fracture. That's several.

Jerry was leaning against the prow rail, scanning the inlets through slitted eyes. He had almost given up hope of ever catching the blackguard when they crested the Chan. Furty wouldn't be in there. You'd want to be an awful eejit to brave the whirlpools in a punt. This thought made Jerry look again. Because, after all, in his opinion, Furty was an awful eejit.

What he saw churned Jerry's stomach more than any seasickness. Holding the rail tightly, he hurried back to the cabin.

"Butterflies!" he blurted breathlessly.

Clipper scowled. "I'm going as fast as I can."

Jerry grabbed the wheel and spun them inland. Right into the mouth of the Chan.

"What are you playing at, Jerry? I'm not going in there! Sure only an eejit would . . ." He paused, obviously arriving at the same conclusion as his friend. Clipper peered through the *Mary Rose*'s weather glass and spotted the punt.

"She's in trouble," he said briskly, reclaiming control of the wheel. "Stand by with the gaff."

Jerry saluted navy style, and pulled the gaff from its holster in the gunwales.

Clipper shifted down to first gear and put the boat side-on into the waves. He judged it perfectly, the bit of forward power and the slap of the waves drawing them alongside the punt in moments. Jerry leaned over the side and hooked the smaller craft's stern rope eye. Furty grabbed the *Mary Rose* with both arms, hauling the keels together.

"Take the girl," he shouted.

Jerry nodded, cradling Babe in his massive hands and lifting her on board. Her pet was in her arms, breathing the quick shallow breaths of the seriously injured. With Babe safely off the punt, Furty swung his legs over the trawler's gunwale and lay gasping on the deck. Clipper pointed a rigid finger at him.

"We'll talk about this later," he promised.

Furty pulled himself on to his knees. "Shaw!" he gasped. "He's still in there. He's hurt."

Clipper paled. "Oh my God. Where is he?"

"There! Between the tall rocks. He's in there!"

Clipper squinted past the spray. The top of Benny's head was barely visible between waves. It flopped weakly in the current.

"Jerry!" said Clipper, a terrified shake in his voice. "Get up on the prow rail. Drag him out of it on the way past. We're only going to have one pass at this."

Jerry nodded, climbing over the cabin on to the rail.

"Be careful up there. I don't want two men overboard." He glared at Furty. "Can you operate a radio?"

Furty nodded, wiping the spray from his brow.

"Call up the coast guard. Tell them we need an airlift to Wexford hospital. Immediately."

Furty ducked into the cabin, and began speaking urgently into the handset.

"And as for you, old girl," Clipper said finally to the boat, "none of your tantrums today. Now's not the time."

Benny was in shock. He had a crushed knee and he was drowning, but he felt grand. A bit groggy maybe, but otherwise fairly okay. His body had wisely decided there was no point in him suffering the pain usually associated with his injuries, and had flooded his brain with endorphins. So for Benny, everything was okeydokey. The water didn't even feel cold anymore.

His thoughts were a bit fuzzy—still there, but sort of out of focus. Except one. The lures. He had to save the lures. And there they were. Right there in the water. All he had to do was let go of this rock and he could reach them. He tried to stand on the ledge, but for some reason he couldn't. Oh, now he remembered. That old engine had crushed his leg. Pity. No more hurling. But at least he'd have the lures.

He caught sight of some fingers wiggling out of the corner of his eye. Were they his own? Nope. His weren't that pudgy. He turned his head slowly to see Jerry straining to reach him.

"Butterflies," grunted Jerry, the prow rail bending under his weight.

Benny smiled, water trickling between his teeth. "Jus' a sec, Jerry. Get these lures."

A wave crashed in, snapping his head back. More salt water wormed its way into his lungs. When his vision cleared Jerry was still there, his face red with effort.

"Butterflies," he pleaded, willing Benny to take his hand.

"I've nearly got 'em. One sec."

Jerry spoke slowly and distinctly. "Benny," he said. "Benny, please."

Benny blinked. Benny, please? That wasn't "butterflies." Who said that? He stared at his Granda's friend. Tears were rolling down the big fellow's cheeks.

"Benny," he said again, stretching out his hand. "Please."

Benny shrugged. How could you refuse an offer like that, from a person who hadn't spoken two different words in forty years. He let go of the rock, and with the last ounce of strength in his good leg, propelled himself into Jerry's waiting arms.

IO
HELL TO PAY

Benny had a few regrets about that day in August. Firstly, he was disgusted about being unconscious for the helicopter ride. Imagine being strapped to the outside of the air-sea rescue chopper, and you snoring away through it all.

Then there was the hurling. He wouldn't be playing for a while, not with a steel pin holding his knee joint together. A couple of the lads had dropped by the hospital with a can of motor oil for his leg. He'd chortled away at the time, but afterward hurled the can from him, sending it skittering across the ward tiles.

He regretted it all being his own fault. It took the good out of getting pampered when he'd brought all this upon himself. Eventually, there'd be hell to pay. And he'd be getting the bill. Oh, everyone smiled and told him not to worry about anything except getting better. But he could see it in their eyes. The disappointment. The betrayal. Especially Granda. He'd only imposed one rule in return for his hospitality. And Benny had managed to break that in to smithereens, pretty much like his knee.

But his biggest regret was Babe. He'd destroyed her faith in him forever. His stubbornness had almost got both of them killed. And for what? For a few lousy baits.

How must she have felt watching him choosing that tin over his own life? What did that say about him? Not a whole lot.

Babe hadn't visited him in hospital. Not once in four months. Not in sixteen agonizing weeks while he was stranded in that lonely bed. At first, Benny told himself that she was just angry with him. Tomorrow. She'll be here tomorrow. But tomorrow came, and Babe didn't. Eventually Benny had to face facts. Babe had taken a glimpse at what he was really like, and decided there was no room for someone like that in her life. You couldn't blame her. Not for a second.

So Benny gritted his teeth and got on with his rehabilitation. The physical therapist was a hulking Kerryman who did not appreciate Benny's disparaging comments about his county's hurling prowess, and seemed to take a malicious glee in straightening the Wexford boy's knee. Whatever Da's eventual punishment was, it couldn't be worse than those afternoons learning to walk down the hospital corridors.

Benny tried everything to avoid having to read. He

watched Australian soaps, he went on long trips around the hospital in his wheelchair, until he was banned from the lifts. He even played "Guess the Disease" with the other ward patients. But eventually he was so brain-numbingly bored, he picked up one of the paperbacks Georgie had brought for him. In spite of himself, Benny found that he enjoyed the antics of Jupiter Jones and the Three Investigators. And when Georgie arrived that night, Benny muttered that he wouldn't be too upset if he had to read another book in the series.

After two months, they took his leg brace off, leaving only a pin sticking out of the side of his knee. Benny hated that pin. It was what stood between him and the hurling pitch. This, Benny told himself, was the reason he was in such foul humor all the time. But that was only partly true. Babe was the real reason.

Eventually they let him home. Benny suspected it was more a case of being kicked out than released. He heard rumors of a planned staff party on the evening of his departure. Usually this would have cheered him up no end, but lately, annoying people wasn't as satisfying as it used to be.

So life returned to normal, with a few glaring exceptions. One, he couldn't run or do anything remotely athletic. Two, the rest of his class had been learning French, and he had no clue what they were talking about. And finally, for the first time in his life, Benny found that he was constantly thinking about someone besides himself.

Benny was lounging on the sofa watching a video of the '96 All Ireland. At least he had access to a remote control at home, which meant that he'd never have to resort to reading again. He was milking the knee injury for a bit of sympathy, even though it rarely gave him more than a twinge these days.

"Mam," he called weakly.

Jessica left whatever she was doing to tend to her eldest. "Yes, Bernard? What is it this time?" Her tones were testy. Maybe he was pushing her too far. "Maybe I could plump your pillows? Or perhaps I could crochet you a head rest? I know, I'll throw a bucket of cold water over you, and maybe you might rouse yourself out of this sulk that you're always in."

"Sorry, Mam," mumbled Benny. "I don't know what's wrong with me."

Jessica sat beside him on the couch, brushing the hair from his eyes. "You have to get on with life, Bernard. Learn from your mistakes."

Benny flicked the pin in his leg. It pinged like a tuning fork. "It's a bit late for that, Mam."

"Don't be silly. The doctors said that you'll be right as rain in six months."

"Six months!" said Benny. "I'll miss the whole season."

"It could have been a lot worse," Jessica reminded him somberly.

Benny shuddered. Ma was right. It could have been a whole lot worse. If it hadn't been for Jerry expanding his vocabulary . . . well, who knows?

The doorbell rang.

"That'll be your grandfather. He gave me a buzz earlier."

Benny was in two minds about seeing Granda. Of course he wanted to see him, but there was still a touch of guilt over getting Clipper's punt wrecked.

Granda came in smiling, his captain's hat pushed back on his forehead. "How's Long John Silver?" he asked, nodding at the knee.

"Not too bad."

"Yer Da tells me the prognosis is better than we thought."

"Yep. I'll be back on the field in six months."

Granda screwed a cigarette into the corner of his mouth. "You got off light, so."

"Light?"

"Well, look what happened to Furty's mother, and she was only doing the garden."

"I suppose. How's he getting on, anyway?"

Granda smiled. "Great. Clipper took him on, seeing as he did such a sterling job steering the punt. He'll be paying for a new propeller out of his wages, by the way."

"After all the complaining I did about him . . ."

"You never know with people. The very one that folks wouldn't give the time of day to . . ."

"And Jerry? How's he?"

Granda opened the sitting-room window and blew a mouthful of smoke through the crack. "Jerry?" he laughed. "You've a lot to answer for there, Benny boy. That chap hasn't said a word but Benny since the accident. It's Benny this, and Benny that. It's driving me mental. No offense, but I think I preferred 'butterflies'."

Benny took a deep breath. "Granda?"

"Yes, Bosun?"

"Will it be all right for me to come down next summer?"

Paddy Shaw thought for a moment. "I suppose so. If you can stand the ridicule. The boys will have a field day with this one. They're already calling you the Black Chicken."

"Do you think Babe will ever talk to me again?"

Granda fired the butt of his cigarette into the garden. "Well now, there's something I can help you with."

"What?"

"She's outside in the car."

Benny's Adam's apple expanded to fill his throat. "What? Your car? This minute?"

Granda nodded, waving any remaining smoke out the window. "I'll get her. Don't run away, now. Ha ha!"

Before Benny could object, Granda was gone. Benny adjusted himself on the couch, hurriedly stuffing a bag of pink marshmallows under a cushion.

Babe entered the room at speed. One got the impression that she'd had a bit of help—a gentle push from a certain lighthouse keeper perhaps. They both stared at the carpet intently for several moments, until Benny eventually broke the silence.

"Howye?" A tentative start. Unemotional, yet friendly.

"Fine," mumbled Babe.

It was hard to judge her mood from that one. Could be too shy to talk. More than likely too angry to say anything.

"You look different."

It was true. She did. Babe had sprouted a few inches. A new hairstyle, shorter but nice, and a Presentation Convent uniform. "You're in school in Wexford now?"

"Yep."

"That's . . . ah . . . great." Benny couldn't get too excited about school. "Me, too. In school in Wexford, I mean. Not in the Presentation."

"I'm in no mood for your jokes, Benny."

That was a pretty definite mood indicator. Fed up. Big time.

"Sorry."

The floodgates were open now. "You're always sorry, townie. I'm sick of listening to you saying you're sorry. I didn't want to come here at all, you know. The Captain hijacked me after class."

"Oh."

"Oh? Is that it? All you can say? Don't you have anything else to say to me?"

Benny was stumped. He was thinking of saying sorry, but Babe obviously didn't want to hear that. He wasn't used to being in this situation. If this had been someone else yelling at him like this, Benny would either have issued a few punches, or else switched off his brain altogether. But all he could do was sit there and listen to this abuse being heaped on him. And he couldn't even run away.

"I don't know, Babe. I don't even remember most of it."

Babe wasn't accepting that as an excuse. "Well, I do. I remember every second, and let me tell you another—"

Benny sneaked a peek to see why the pixie had stopped her tirade. She was staring at his knee, and the pin sticking out of it.

"Sore, is it?"

Benny shrugged heroically. "Sometimes. At night, you know."

"Good enough for you."

"I got off light."

"Certainly did. We could all have been killed."

Babe strolled over and caught hold of the pin. "Would it hurt, now, if I was to give this a twist?"

"It might," stammered Benny.

"Do you think, now, that you deserve a little twist for making me watch my best friend trying to kill himself over a box of lures?"

"Your best friend?"

"You used to be. I don't know about now."

Benny was surprised to feel his heart speed up. It was nothing to do with Babe's threat, either. "Babe."

"Just shut up. I don't want to hear it, whatever it is."

"Babe, listen."

Babe tightened her grip on the pin. "Shut up. I'm warning you."

"Babe, that day, in the Chan. It was the worst, dopiest thing I've ever done. The whole idea. The bait war thing. All my stupid fault."

"Tell me something I don't know."

Benny paused. He had to say something really special here. Something that Georgie might say. Girls liked that sort of thing. And looking at Babe now, she was definitely a girl. One hundred percent. But whatever he came up with had to be true. He knew from bitter experience with his Ma that females could spot a fib a mile away. "Do you know the worst thing about that day?"

"Losing your lures, was it?"

"No," said Benny, praying he could make it through the next sentence without dissolving into hysterical laughter. "The worst thing wasn't the leg getting battered, or nearly drowning, or Clipper's engine getting crocked." Babe was listening now, waiting for the punchline. "It was letting you down, Babe. Letting down my best friend."

Benny gazed at the carpet. He'd said it now, that was all he could do. A bit heavy on the wobbly voice, maybe, but it was too late to change that now.

He chanced a look at his old partner. Babe was doing her utmost to maintain an unforgiving face, but her mask was cracking.

"You did let me down, townie."

"I know. I'm . . ."

"Don't say it."

"But I am sorry. I am."

Babe sighed. "So, Benny. What are we going to do? There's no point having a partner who's going to go around apologizing all the time. It's pathetic."

Benny grinned. "I know."

"And you're going to be useless over the rocks with that gammy leg."

"I'll be grand by July. No problem."

"Hmm. I suppose I could give you one more chance."

"Really?"

"The Black Chicken clucks again."

"I'm going to have to listen to this all summer, am I?"

Babe smiled nastily. "That's not all. There's a little matter of a twist on this pin here."

Benny swallowed. "You're having me on, right?"

"Am I?"

"Ah, Babe. There's no need for violence."

"There's every need. I have to be sure you're really sorry."

"I am, honest to God."

Babe curled her fingers around the pin. "There's only one way to find out."

She gritted her teeth and wrenched. Benny screamed like a pinched baby.

"Sucker!" gloated Babe, who, of course, hadn't twisted it at all.

Benny took several deep breaths. This, he realized dismally, was only the beginning. Babe would be making him pay for last summer for a very long time.

Jessica eyed Paddy Shaw suspiciously. "Were you smoking in my house?"

Granda smiled innocently. "Me? God, no. I'd never dream of it."

Jessica stared into his eyes. "Paddy?"

"All right, just one little roll-up, but I was over by the window. Swear."

"You know the rule. There are young lungs in this house."

"Okay," said Granda humbly. "Sorry, Jessie girl."

The interrogation was interrupted by a piercing scream from the sitting room.

"Oh my Lord!" gasped Jessica, hurrying to the door. "What's going on in there?"

Granda smiled. "Leave them, Jessica. I think our Benny's finally starting to pay for his crimes." He winked broadly. "I warned him never to get on the wrong side of Babe Meara."